SHADOWS OF THE HEART

AN URBAN FANTASY THRILLER

CECILIA DOMINIC

DEDICATION

Writing this novel in the spring of 2020 helped me to escape from the world and the difficult situation of the pandemic. It also allowed me to attend a fantasy conference, if only in my imagination. I had originally planned this novel to come out just before DragonCon, which moved virtual, as so many other 'Cons did. DragonCon is also the highlight of my year as a fantasy author, my best chance to hang out with my fellow writers and see my fans face-to-face. I especially missed drinks at the Westin bar with my author friends and talking to my fans after panels.

Consequently, this book is dedicated to my fellow nerds, geeks, and fantasy and science fiction fans who missed the chance to gather with their kindred spirits, talk about their favorite books and other media, and show off their costumes. I hope you stay healthy and sane, and here's hoping we can all come together again in 2021 and beyond.

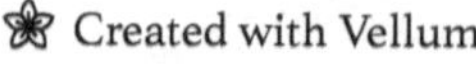 Created with Vellum

LOOK FOR THESE OTHER TITLES BY CECILIA DOMINIC:

Urban Fantasy Series:

The Lycanthropy Files
The Wolf's Shadow
Long Shadows
Blood's Shadow
A Million Shadows

The Fae Files
The Shadow Project
Shadows of the Heart
The Shadowed Path
Shadows of the Sky
Rising Shadows (autumn 2022)
Shadows of the Past (early 2023)

Dream Weavers & Truth Seekers
Perchance to Dream
Truth Seeker
Tangled Dreams

Web of Truth

Steampunk Series:

The Aether Psychics
Noble Secrets
Eros Element
Clockwork Phantom
Aether Spirit
Aether Rising

The Inspector Davidson Mysteries
The Art of Piracy
Mission: Nutcracker

1

REINE

"'Ello, sis," the scarred Fae prince greeted me.

"Oh, no. It's my brother," I murmured to Lawrence before forcing a smile and exclaiming, "Rhys!"

Sir Raleigh's weight disappeared from my shoulder. I knew the cat would be back, so I didn't think anything of it and instead turned my attention to my not-so-long-lost brother. If this was my mother's idea of help, I had to question whose side she was on.

Rhys moved up the hill toward us, his actions lithe and precise. He'd still not learned to move like a human. It was like watching the difference between a domesticated dog and a coyote. I made a mental note to mention that to him—he'd need to blend in.

Oh, Hades, this was a mess. But it wasn't like I could send him back.

The ground under our feet rumbled, and a shock of electric energy went through me. *"Welcome, sister and brother,"* the spirit of the hill said, more clearly than I had heard it previously. *"I am honored to host two royal Fae."*

Interesting. Even exiles deserved honor, I guessed.

Rhys and I both bowed, which meant I had a confused gargoyle by my side. In fact, as soon as Rhys had greeted me, Lawrence's brows had drawn together and his lips had tightened in a perplexed frown. I'd have to tease him about his stoneface later. If he would accept teasing.

I'd left things in a mess earlier. He didn't know I'd been about to head back to Faerie without saying goodbye.

"How did you get here?" I asked Rhys.

Instead of answering, he raised his eyebrows and inclined his head toward Lawrence. "Who's your friend?" His nostrils flared, which I knew was for show. Rhys could tell what kind of paranormal creature someone was by reading their energy, like I could. "Your *gargoyle* friend?"

Lawrence tensed, and I squeezed his arm. "This is Doctor Lawrence Gordon. He's part of the Center for Paranormal Disease Control and Prevention. Lawrence, this is my brother Rhys."

Rhys narrowed his eyes. "You look familiar, mate. Have we met?"

"Not that I'm aware of," Lawrence replied, his voice low and tense.

Neither of them moved to shake hands. The air between them held the repellent tension of two magnets turned toward each other with the same pole.

"Well, then, we'll have to catch up later," I said to Rhys. "We have a problem."

"So I hear."

Rhys fell into step on my other side from Lawrence as we descended the mountain. I decided to skip the gondolas. It seemed a bad idea to have the two men in the same enclosed space. We'd deal with the hotel elevators later. Plus, at least at this early time of the morning, with the rising sun still making long shadows on the path, we were alone. I couldn't sense anyone else, human or paranormal. Even the ghosts had cleared out. Or maybe they'd gone dormant. Every creature, living and dead, had its own rhythm, and even a Fae wouldn't know all of them.

Or... Rhys' energy had a certain wildness to it, as he hadn't embraced life in the human realm as I had. I'd had it easier, but what had I lost touch with?

"You're lost in your thoughts, Sis," Rhys teased. "You going to tell me what we're up against?"

Before I could respond, Lawrence stopped, and I skidded to a halt beside him.

"You two go ahead," he said. "I'm not feeling up for this right now. I'll take the gondola down. Meet you at the bottom?"

"I have a car," Rhys said. "I'll take her back to the hotel since you're too weak. Go on ahead and take a nap."

Lawrence advanced, his right hand clenched into a fist, and I put a hand on his chest.

I looked over my shoulder at my brother as I held Lawrence back. "Gods, Rhys, you can't help yourself, can you? In the past few days, Lawrence has been poisoned and then attacked by the soul-eater. If he's not at his full strength, he's got reasons."

"Soul-eater, eh?" Rhys shrugged. "Fine. I take it back. Well, except for the part about bringing my sister back to the hotel." The glare he gave Lawrence would have made for a comical, *"I'm defending my sister's honor,"* moment in any other circumstances. I bit my tongue—literally—before I could tell Rhys that Lawrence and I had spent the night together. True, nothing had happened, but he didn't need to know that. He didn't need to know anything, really. In fact, the less he knew about my current life, the better.

At that moment, Sir Raleigh, my kitten-shaped grimalkin, reappeared. He had an aura of cold around him, and his fur chilled my neck as he draped himself over my shoulders.

"And where have you been, wee lad?" I asked. He didn't

typically go away for so long when he disappeared. I'd have to ponder that later.

"Are you all right with this plan, Reine?" Lawrence asked. Poor guy, he did have dark circles under his eyes. He put a hand on my upper arm, and I sensed his reluctance to leave me and concern I'd disappear again.

Yeah, that had been a dick move on my part, sneaking out of his bed. Even if I didn't have a dick, I could act like one sometimes. Like my brother.

"I am. I'll see you back at the hotel. I promise."

"Right, be careful."

Half-hoping he'd reappear and ask me to come with him, I watched until he disappeared around a bend in the wooded path.

Rhys didn't wait even a minute before he asked, "A gargoyle? Really, Reine? You know—"

"Yes, I know. Traditional enemy. One helped maim you. Blah blah blah." I put my hands on my hips. "But this one is a good one."

"No such thing." He shrugged and started walking down the mountain again.

I followed him. "I guess we'll have to agree to disagree on this one." *Like most everything else.*

What was my mother up to? Most obvious explanation— this was a way to get my brother in on my chance to return home so my grandmother would make an exception to the "perfect Fae only" rule and allow him with his scarred cheek back into Faerie. Mother had always liked him better.

But then, wasn't there always another layer with the Fae? We didn't just do subplots and subterfuge—we wove in hidden motivations, loopholes, and a good measure of deception.

Whatever her motivation, I had no doubt Rhys would only get in my way.

The sun had risen further and added a dappled overlay to

the rocky path. We focused on where we put our feet until we got to a smoother stretch.

Be nice, be nice, be nice... "If you're going to help me, you need to know what's up."

"Apparently, especially since you're keeping company with a gargoyle and a grimalkin."

Sir Raleigh chirped, and I smiled and scratched him behind one ear. His purr rumbled into my shoulders and reminded me to relax them.

"There's a soul-eater on the loose. It first attacked me in my cottage and followed me here. It's getting stronger, has already taken over and killed a couple of people."

I expected Rhys to make some sort of wisecrack or dismissive statement, but he thought for a moment and asked, "How could it have attacked you in your cottage? You have strong wards around it."

"It took over a bird I was feeding, and I invited it in."

"Rookie mistake, sis."

"It was a bird, Rhys."

"Human mistake, then."

My cheeks heated with a blush. "What's that supposed to mean?"

"No wonder you're in trouble. We Fae don't trust anyone or anything. What about that ridiculous creature on your shoulders?"

Sir Raleigh had twisted so his chest faced out, and he hung with his paws stretched over his head and alongside his tail. I resisted the urge to take my phone out and take a cat-stole selfie. Instead, I rubbed the soft gray fur on his chest, and he kneaded the air. His one white paw, the front left one, revealed sharp claws.

"I don't know. He came to me the same day I was attacked, but before. He can sense it even when I can't, so he's helpful."

"Do you know who sent him?"

"No." And I wondered whether his relatively long absence indicated he'd gone to give someone a report about Rhys appearing. "But he defended me, so I think he's on our side."

Rhys didn't appear convinced, and I read the censure that I hadn't been Fae enough in his expression. "You're going soft, sis."

I put on some Fae speed and whipped around him, placing one hand on his chest and the other at his throat. His momentum made me slide backward, but I held on. "Don't ever say anything like that to me." I squeezed, and he put his hands to mine, but I gathered energy from the mountain I stood on and paralyzed him. His face turned red, and his eyes widened. Although I didn't match his height, I was not a small Fae. Nor was I a weak one, even though being so far from home attenuated my powers. He'd made the mistake to insult me in the one place where I could act closer to my full strength.

"And while I have your attention," I continued, "this is how things are going to go. I'm in charge. Every time you've gone off and done your own thing, it's ended in disaster. This time, you take orders, don't argue, and behave. Is that clear?" I loosened the spell and my grip just enough for him to nod. Then I released him and stepped aside as he fell to his hands and knees. He gasped in a few breaths, then looked up at me. Respect and fear had replaced the skepticism in his eyes, but his next words made me feel worse, not better.

"You remind me of Mum sometimes."

I closed my eyes and took a deep breath. "I'll accept that as a compliment just this once."

He staggered to his feet and gripped a tree, taking another couple of breaths before straightening all the way. I could tell his powers were also less than usual, likely for the same reason I struggled—Fae were tied to place as a source of strength, and ours was the underground caves in Scotland.

"But I do need to warn you of something," Rhys told me. "I do know that gargoyle from somewhere. And I haven't seen that many."

It would be my bad luck if Lawrence had somehow been involved in Rhys's maiming, but I shrugged, not letting my fear show. "Let me know when you figure it out."

~

RHYS'S CAR turned out to be a black, low-slung, two-seater convertible. What was it with paranormal men and their convertibles? Not that I could say much about impractical vehicles—I rode a motorcycle, which was currently being repaired back in Scotland.

We arrived at the hotel to find Lawrence waiting for us by the front door. Others wouldn't have been able to tell, but I saw relief flicker across his face. Guilt again stabbed me, but I mentally swatted it away. Rhys had reminded me—I needed to act like the Fae I was if I was going to survive this thing and return home.

Lawrence opened my car door like a gentleman, and we stepped to the side while Rhys gave very specific instructions to the valets. How had Rhys scored a luxury vehicle? When Mother had sent me to Atlanta earlier that week—which felt like a century ago—I'd been on my own and dependent on the kindness of strangers. Well, and my rideshare apps that mysteriously never ran out of money. I missed having the freedom of my own transportation, but I didn't trust myself to drive on the right side of the road in the States.

"Are you all right?" Lawrence asked.

"Yes." I reached to my shoulder, and Sir Raleigh pushed his head under my hand with an emphatic purr. "Rhys can't hurt me. I've always been the stronger of the two of us."

"I don't mean physically." Lawrence's face still had his stony gargoyle expression, and he narrowed his gray eyes at Rhys. Huh. I hadn't seen that reaction from him before, but then, we'd only known each other for a couple of days.

"I'm fine." I didn't know what else to say. Not here, anyway, with lots of curious eyes watching and ears listening. And there did seem to be a lot of people around. Was the hotel a busy place on Fridays? I didn't think a shopping mall could draw that many people from out of town.

"I don't know if I believe you. We have a lot to talk about." Lawrence crossed his arms. "Like why did you sneak away this morning? Did I do something to anger you?"

Gods, is that what he thought of me? That I'd leave in a snit after he'd been injured and had lost one of his friends?

"No, not at all. I had to go meet my mother, and..." I shrugged. "Fae business. I didn't want to wake you."

A half-truth. I hadn't wanted to wake him so I could avoid the pain of saying goodbye. When I'd left the hotel that morning, I'd thought Sir Raleigh and I had a ticket to Faerie. Of course, I hadn't. I still had to settle the one hanging thread of a monster, who hopefully should still be dormant after its activities of the previous evening.

"Right."

I could tell he didn't believe me. He'd already caught me in one deception when I hadn't told him I'd searched his lab.

Rhys walked over to us. He had a black faux leather duffel bag slung over one shoulder, and his half-grin told me he'd heard at least some of our discussion. Damn that Fae hearing.

"I hope there's a room for me. This is a busy place."

A porter pushed a luggage rack full of suitcases and boxes past us, and a sparkling object caught my eye—a pair of strap-on wings. What in the world?

"Excuse me," I asked him. "What's going on here?"

The man stopped and grinned. What could he find so funny? Oh, Hades, I had tucked my hair behind one pointed ear to get it out of Sir Raleigh's face. Then the man looked at Rhys, whose ears, of course, were on full display. Yet another thing I'd have to talk to him about—hide the damn things with a spell or something.

"Nice costumes, Miss, Sir. I swear, y'all start dressing up earlier every year."

"What?"

He pointed to a stand-up sign I hadn't noticed. It read, "Welcome to Fae-Con" and had instructions on where to check in for the hotel and the 'Con.

"Oh, right." I gave him what I hoped was a dazzling smile, but without any kind of charm or push behind it.

He glanced around and dropped his volume. "You may want to hide the cat, though. The manager doesn't allow pets in public spaces."

"Right, thanks."

The porter nodded and continued along.

"Well, you should fit right in," Lawrence said too cheerfully. "Shall we see about getting your brother a room?"

Luckily, they had one available two floors below ours. I noticed Lawrence didn't offer to trade with him, and that gave me hope. Perhaps he wanted to stay close to me.

Or maybe he took his job of protecting me seriously.

I puzzled over his logic as we lined up to wait for the elevator.

Rhys frowned at the crowd. "I'll take the stairs, thanks." He walked away before I could argue with him. I started after him, but Lawrence grabbed my arm.

"Don't worry about him. How much trouble could he possibly get into?"

I arched an eyebrow. "You have no idea. I'll fill you in later." But I decided to wait with him. I hated the metal boxes, but I'd just gotten a nice recharge from Stone Mountain, so I decided to remain with Lawrence.

One of the four cars filled up, and we moved forward. A young woman next to me bumped into me, and I tried to move away from her, which meant I nudged Lawrence and lost my balance. He steadied me with a hand on my arm, which was a good thing. Sir Raleigh growled just before the girl leaned over, and her eyes flashed yellow.

Hades. The soul-eater had found me.

The young woman's mouth split into an evil smile that didn't belong on her pretty face and said, "You can try to hide, but I'll find you. I'll get you. Just wait."

"That's what you think." Right, next task—find new hotel.

As if the soul-eater could read my mind, it added, "And if you move out of the hotel, I'll take my revenge on your friends and the innocents here."

She clasped my wrist, and my knees went weak. Then the girl's eyes rolled up, and she fainted. I managed to catch her and lower her to the floor as the people around us stepped back, juggling their luggage. I put my hand to her neck and found her pulse to be strong.

A short man with a terrier-like face and black eyes rushed over. He had a radio clipped to his belt, and he ran a hand through his thinning dark hair.

"What happened?" he snapped. He sounded more annoyed than concerned, which made me respond more harshly than I should.

"She fainted, you idiot. Do you have some sort of medical personnel here?"

He sneered at me. "Of course. Everyone step back, give her some air."

We managed to get the girl out of the elevator line and to a couch in the lobby, and a medical crew arrived with a blood pressure cuff, oxygen, and other equipment. Once I confirmed they knew what they were doing, Lawrence and I left, but I couldn't stop shivering, my mind whirling with panic now that I didn't have to worry about the girl who'd been taken over.

The problem had reached a whole new level—the soul-eater was stalking the convention.

2

REINE

I didn't stop shaking, even when Lawrence and I arrived at our joined rooms. He sat with me on the bed and rubbed my shoulders and upper arms until I stilled, and then I leaned against him, my head on his shoulder.

"What happened?" he asked. "I couldn't hear what she said to you."

"It was the soul-eater." Every time I blinked I saw the girl's eyes go yellow as it took her over. "It told me it's here, and it's going to get me. And if I try to change hotels, it will go after you, Selene, and Corey as well as the 'Con." I straightened and leaned back to see his face. "Lawrence, all these people are in danger. Who knows who it will use as a conduit to try to come after me?"

"Why doesn't it attack you directly?" Lawrence asked.

"When she grabbed me, I caught a flash of its intent. It wants to toy with me, weaken me." Ugh, typical Fae strategy—play with the prey before pouncing. "If I hadn't just been to Stone Mountain and filled up on the energy..."

"...and recharged your Earth elemental side..." Lawrence

brushed a tear from my cheek. "It will be okay. You're stronger than you think."

He, of course, had no idea of the secret I had been charged to keep. Rather than having only earth, water, and air elements as others thought, the Fae had all five, including fire and spirit. Plus, we could draw from all of them and change the nature of matter. I let him continue to think we were limited to three.

"I don't know." I'd done a cowardly thing that morning when I had sneaked out. "But we need to figure out how to stop the 'Con."

"I'll call John." He grimaced, and I winced as well at the thought. "As much as I hate to do it, he's the one with the authority. Even if he woke this morning without his wife beside him."

I chose not to take that as a dig. "He'll understand."

Lawrence pulled out his phone and called John Graves, now the acting head of the CPDC with Lucius Cimex having been arrested for shooting John's wife, Beverly. That's how the government went—keep the chain of succession in spite of personal hardship.

John picked up on the second ring. "Lawrence, thank gods. Do you know where Kestrel is?"

"Hey, John, I have you on speaker. I'm here with Doctor River, and no, we don't know where your daughter is." Lawrence and I exchanged concerned looks. "Is she missing?"

"Yes, since early this morning. I've called Corey."

"We'll help search for her, but I have another concern." He explained about Fae-Con and the soul-eater. "Who knows how much damage this thing could inflict?"

A pause, during which I clenched my fists. Was John seriously considering whether we had a valid reason for calling off Fae-Con? I reminded myself that humans' brains didn't think straight when grief was involved, so maybe he needed more time to process.

"I think you're right," John finally said. "And I think it may be cleverer than Doctor River has given it credit for. I sent the wine from last night's office happy hour for analysis to see if anything had been put in it."

"And...?" I asked.

"Still waiting for results. But I had to find out what got into Lucius."

I thought the answer to that was easy and as old as humanity itself. Lucius Cimex had had an unrequited—as far as we knew—crush on Beverly Graves and then shot her so she couldn't expose his involvement in the true Shadow Project, an effort to sample and map the DNA of paranormal creatures, including me. I didn't share my thoughts. There would be time for recriminations later. If John needed denial about his friend and mentor right now, he could have it.

"Back to the soul-eater," Lawrence said. "Who do we talk to?"

"The 'Con is run by a couple, but I don't know their names. Kestrel would—this is one of her regular 'Cons, although she was skipping this year because of school demands. You could probably ask at the registration desk, but since they don't know of us and what we do, it could be a hard sell."

"Right, who's going to believe a story about an invisible monster?" I asked.

"The other option is the hotel manager. We've got a good working relationship with the hotel, or at least we did. The manager is new this quarter, and we haven't had much luck with him."

"What do you mean?" Lawrence asked.

A sigh. "He's pushed back on everything we've asked him to do. Those adjoining rooms you're in and that Doctor Rial and Corey have down the hall? If they hadn't already been available, I don't know that we could have gotten him to move people."

Ugh, I hated difficult humans. "That's not promising."

"No. He hasn't had to handle a supernatural crisis yet. They always come around after their first exorcism."

"And this is way worse." I flopped back on the bed. "Well, we can only try. What's his name?"

"James Leak."

I sat, the memory of the terrier-man's brass nametag flashing into my brain. "Crap."

"What?" John and Lawrence both asked.

"I just called that guy an idiot."

LAWRENCE and I hung up with John with another promise to search for Kestrel after we talked to James Leak about shutting down the 'Con. The front desk staff directed us to an office on the tier below the main conference and hotel lobby level. Whereas the four-story glass windows facing the wooded area had formerly given the space an open, natural feel, they now made me feel exposed. I directed my attention to the stairs in front of me instead of outside.

We found the office, and Lawrence knocked.

"Come in!" the man from earlier barked.

This was not going to be easy. Indeed, he frowned when he saw us.

"You two again? What, has someone else fainted?"

"How is the girl?" I asked.

"Fine. She just got overheated. Corset was too tight." He dismissed her with a wave of his hand. "No big deal."

"We actually have a different explanation," Lawrence said. "We're with the CPDC."

Leak's eyebrows rose. "The who? Oh right, the ghostbusters. They told me about you."

Lawrence didn't react to the dig. He continued calmly, "We

handle more than just spirits who have lingered after their bodies have been removed, and we have a concern."

"It's actually more of a situation," I said.

Leak smirked at me. "Right, I'm sure. More than a girl who got dehydrated?"

"You just said overheated," I pointed out. Lawrence nudged me.

"Whatever. There was nothing seriously wrong with her. She said she was waiting in line, then felt dizzy, and the next thing she knew, she was waking up on the couch in the lobby." He shrugged, palm-up. "I don't know why you're making such a big deal of it. Unless you think there's something...supernatural...going on." He wiggled his fingers.

I guessed that was supposed to be ghostly?

"The girl didn't faint because of her corset or anything else mundane," Lawrence said. "Just before she went under, something spoke through her to my colleague."

"Oh?" Leak sat back. "Do tell. What did it say? 'I'll get you, my pretty'?"

"Something like that."

"Come now, Miss...?"

"Doctor River, actually."

"Right, Doctor River. If I'm going to help you, I need to know exactly what happened."

I took a deep breath. "It said, 'You can try to hide, but I'll find you. I'll get you. Just wait.'"

"But it didn't do anything to you?"

"I don't know." The wave of weakness had passed, and I didn't know whether it had been due to the fright or something else. I didn't want to believe the soul-eater could suck my energy like that, but it would make sense.

"And do you know what this alleged *something* wants to do to you? Why it threatened you?"

"No," Lawrence told him, "but we know it's dangerous. It's killed before."

Leak paused for a long moment, then asked, "Do you have autopsy reports—death by invisible body-taking-over creature?" The corners of his mouth twitched, and I could tell he didn't believe a word we'd said.

"Look, Mr. Leak—"

"You can call me Jimmy. Not sure about *Doctor* River over there. And you are...?"

"Doctor Lawrence Gordon."

"Great." He sighed like our titles annoyed him. "Right, so the two of you think you're so smart and you bring me a story of an invisible creature that may or may not be a threat. Do you know how many people are depending on this hotel to host Fae-Con and have a good time this weekend? About a thousand. And do you know how much money we'll lose if we just call it off? Several times that. So no, I can't do anything unless you bring me something concrete."

"Mr. Leak," I said, putting a little Fae persuasion behind my words, "I understand your concerns, but think about how much money it will cost if the hotel is sued over someone getting hurt or killed here. The soul-eater is clever. It won't make anything obvious except to me."

He blinked, and I sensed that my persuasion, which hadn't penetrated his thick, concrete psyche, fell away from him like water off a siren's tail. "I still need proof, Doctor River. My bosses aren't going to be happy if I cancel Fae-Con, even if it's for a fairy tale." He laughed at his joke, and it came out as a wheezing sound. "Meanwhile, I hope the two of you enjoy your weekend."

Lawrence's eyes had gone dark, and I hoped he wasn't about to gargoyle out in here, although I'd thoroughly enjoy seeing Jimmy Leak wet his trousers.

Lawrence drew himself up to his full height and leaned

over the desk. He spoke with quiet firmness that I found rather sexy. "Jimmy, since you can't call off the 'Con, I need you to at least give us access to areas guests usually aren't able to get into."

"On what authority?"

"CPDC. I can call our director right now, and he'll be sure to let your superiors know you've not been helpful."

Another long pause, and then Leak said as though Lawrence hadn't made his suggestion, "If it helps, since you're with the CPDC, I'll give you access to all areas of the hotel. That way you can keep an eye on things, chase your invisible monsters." He handed us both master key cards. "Just don't get in the way of anything. Oh, and Doctor River?" He pointed at Sir Raleigh, who lounged on my shoulder and licked his white paw. "You can't have that...animal...in the public areas. People have allergies."

"Thank you, we'll keep that in mind," Lawrence said.

I nodded. I dared not open my mouth, not even to thank him for the cards, or I'd call him something worse than an idiot.

As soon as we walked out of Leak's office, Lawrence rubbed my back again. The fury at being dismissed melted into annoyance, and I relaxed under his soothing touch.

"How do you do that?" I asked.

"What?" Now he grinned.

"Calm me down by just rubbing my back? Do gargoyles have magic in their hands?" Whoops, I hadn't meant that to come out sounding as it had, and my face heated as my thoughts went to what else Lawrence could do with his hands. I thanked my brain for the ill-timed sex fantasies with all the sarcasm I could muster.

"I'm not going to answer that. You'll have to find out for yourself."

His switch from annoyed gargoyle to flirty and handsome man released tension I hadn't yet recognized, and I squeezed his hand. Then I spotted the young woman who had fainted. She sat with some friends, all wearing medieval-style dresses with corsets, and they all had prosthetic ear tips. They sat around a table in the hotel coffee shop.

"Come on," I told Lawrence. "Let's go talk to her. I want to see if she remembers anything about the soul-eater's intent."

I had taken just two steps in that direction when Lawrence's phone buzzed.

"It's from John. He's asked for an update. Also, if we've gone to help look for Kestrel yet."

"Right." I sighed, not out of annoyance, but more a sense of being overwhelmed. I couldn't take any more emergencies. "Let's do that first. I'll try to call Kestrel."

3

REINE

Kestrel's phone went straight to voice mail. Lawrence made a call of his own and arranged for us to rendezvous with a worried mountain lion shifter who also happened to be the closest thing Kestrel had to a boyfriend. Unfortunately for them, the fact that they were both in the Paranormal Bureau of Investigation, and Kestrel a trainee, made their relationship forbidden.

Corey met us in front of the crystal store where we'd had the seance that had put us in touch with a dark Fae who called himself Troubadour, and who had told us to "ally with fangs." That reminded me—the vampire club co-owner had expressed interest in helping us. She would be a last resort. Vampires rated just above dark Fae on the trustworthy scale, which was to say, almost not trustworthy at all.

The were-lion's dark blond hair stood up from his scalp like he'd been running his hands through it, and his eyes were red-rimmed and sported bags underneath them. A golden layer of stubble lined his face. Worry and sorrow came from him in waves, and I had to stop and ground myself so I could shield against his strong emotions. That I hadn't automatically done so spoke to my own exhaustion. Again—expected or due to the soul-eater's attack?

How could I face an enemy if I didn't know what it was capable of doing?

"Thanks for coming, Doctors," Corey said. "I've gone to all her usual spots. She's not at her parents' house..." He swallowed and rubbed his eyes. "Her father's house. Not at the morgue where they took Beverly's body. Not at her favorite coffee shop or bar..."

"In other words, nowhere she knew you'd search for her." I placed a hand on his arm and found hurt bubbling through his concern and grief. Why hadn't she reached out to him? She'd been angry at all the time he'd had to spend with Selene Rial, who had come with me from Scotland to try to figure out who had leaked top secret information from the CPDC lab. Now we'd both ended up in the middle of a murder investigation and monster hunt.

"Do you think she's all right?" he asked.

"Well, we know who killed Beverly and why, and the soul-eater is after me, so I can't think of why Kestrel would be in danger. Has she run off before?"

"Once, after we had a big fight. She avoided me and her parents for a couple of days." His shoulders relaxed a touch, but I could tell my logic hadn't comforted him overmuch.

Selene emerged from the shop with Aria, the medium who had conducted the séance and the shop's owner. The redheaded Selene looked extra tall next to Aria's petite frame. Aria darted a look between us, her striking gray eyes sharp under her frown.

"There you are," Selene said. "Any luck with the hotel manager?"

"John's been keeping us updated," Corey explained. "If we can find Kestrel, she can introduce you to Fae-Con's directors.

They're friends of hers, and they're more open to the supernatural."

"I'd still help you even if I didn't need Kestrel's connections at Fae-Con," I assured him. "Where was she last seen?"

"She left the lab late last night after the cops questioned her, but before John. He thought she'd gone back to her apartment. He didn't leave the lab until a few hours ago."

"That means he hasn't slept either," Lawrence said. He ducked his head, and I suspected we felt the same thing—guilt over having gotten at least a few hours' sleep, which then continued into more shame for me over my behavior that morning. Rhys's words from earlier came back to me, and I took a deep breath to dispel the feelings. Fae didn't do guilt or shame, especially not royal Fae, and if I was going to make it back to Faerie, I couldn't let such things get in the way of what I needed to do.

First—find Kestrel.

Second—get introduced to the 'Con directors.

Third—convince them to call it off, preferably before more people arrived and gave the soul-eater more bodies to hide in.

Fourth—capture the soul-eater and banish it. Or something. I'd figure that one out once I got there.

Aria spoke. "I can attempt to scry and find her, but she's a talented witch even if her powers haven't settled."

We all winced. Kestrel's powers refusing to settle on a type of magic talent had been one of the main drivers for all the recent troubles.

"Whatever you can do," Corey said. "I'm out of ideas."

"It will help if I have her here." Aria inclined her head toward me. "She's fairly buzzing with magical energy. Although..." Her finely shaped brows drew together. "You seem faded this morning, Doctor River."

"I feel faded," I said with a shrug. "I suspect everyone is after last night."

"Fair." She gestured for us to follow her.

We went through the main shop, where the crystals chimed at me and gave me a little energy, and to the back room. It still had the appearance of a Victorian séance chamber, but today, the table in the middle held a large black stone bowl three quarters full of water.

"Nice smoky quartz bowl," I said. "May I?"

Aria nodded. "Please. I'm honored for any help you can give."

I sat and placed my palms on the outside of the bowl. I inhaled, then softly blew across the surface of the water. I'd only intended to test it, to see how clear visions could be and give it a little extra power for Aria's scrying attempt, but I saw something.

Rhys, dressed in peasant clothing from two centuries back, stood in front of a cottage. He tied a cloth around his face and drew the hood of a cloak over his head. Determination steeled his features, and rage danced in his eyes. He glanced over his shoulder, seemingly right at me, and I gasped and drew back, letting go of the bowl. Water sloshed over the side.

"Are you all right?" Lawrence asked at the same time Corey started forward.

"Did you see Kestrel?" he asked.

"No, no, it was something personal. Something historical." I gave Aria a shaky smile. "Your bowl works. Sorry about the spill."

"That's fine. It's only water." Aria blotted at the tablecloth with a white towel, then surprised me by putting a hand on my arm. "Whatever you saw, it was relevant to you now, even if it happened in the past. I could feel the threads tying past to present."

"You're a powerful witch, then. I didn't feel anything of the sort."

"Or it's something you don't want to know. The mind is often stronger than we think."

"Right." I stood and gestured to the bowl. "I'll get out of the way and let you search for Kestrel, then, since I warmed it up for you."

"Thanks." She sat and held out a hand. Corey reached out a hand, and the dim light glinted off something long and red between his fingertips—a hair, presumably one of Kestrel's.

Aria picked up one of the candles and held the flame to the hair. It burned in a flash of light and acrid-smelling smoke, and the ashes drifted to the surface of the bowl as Aria whispered a finding spell. I had questioned how she could afford to maintain a specialty shop in a neighborhood such as this, and I suspected I now had my answer. If people were hiring her to find their missing loved ones or pets, she'd included a nice service aspect with her business.

Corey started the video function on his phone and murmured, "So we catch all the details."

Aria took a few deep breaths and blew across the surface of the water. As it had with me, it stilled sooner than physics would have dictated, and I resisted the urge to lean and watch over her shoulder.

The medium spoke in a hushed, trance-like tone. "I see an ornate wooden bar. There's some sort of sport on the television —soccer. She's there, sitting at the bar. Stone walls. Sorrow. So much sorrow."

"Can you see anything else that will give us a clue as to the location?" Lawrence asked.

"There are images with shamrocks. Celtic writing." Her lips curled into a moue. "Funny sayings about Irish things." Aria gasped and slumped back, then rubbed her eyes before opening them. "That's all I could see. Did it help?"

"Sounds like she's in a pub," I said. "An Irish pub. Do you have a lot of those here in Atlanta?"

"A few." Corey ran his hand through his hair again. The gesture didn't help its dishevelment and moved his overall demeanor down the scale away from apex predator and toward scruffy housecat. "We'll check them out and see."

Lawrence had his phone out. "I can narrow it down to two."

"How?" Corey asked.

"It's early for soccer here. That means it must be one of the European leagues, and only a couple of places opened to show them. One of them is nearby."

"Great," Selene said. "I promised John I'd be at the lab today, be available for anyone who needs to talk. Call me if you need me."

"You're okay going alone?" Corey asked. He sounded conflicted.

"Yes, I'll be fine. I'll call if I get in trouble."

So that left us three. Aria needed to tend her shop. We piled into Corey's truck so we wouldn't have to deal with parking two cars and went on our witch hunt.

A Fae, a gargoyle, and a were-lion walked into a bar...

...without a grimalkin, who had remained in the truck since most restaurants didn't allow animals.

I didn't know what to expect when we entered the pub in downtown Decatur. Just as Aria had said, lovely woodworking made the bar distinctive. It resembled something out of a Georgian hallway, although obviously it couldn't have been that old. Stone walls, another check, as were the Irish signs and sayings.

The place was half-full, which still meant a lot of people for that time in the morning. We couldn't see all of the seats, so we wove through small groups standing around and near the bar. Tiny figures chased a round, black and white ball across a green field on the television, and I jumped when the place erupted in cheers and groans as the ball went into a net.

"Do you follow the game?" Lawrence asked me.

"No, which I'm sure makes me a bad Scot. I never bothered to take the time to understand the subtleties." Indeed, I didn't care for sports. The passion they incited reminded me too much of the atmosphere of a village before its men went to war. I granted the humans their substitutes, but I'd never liked that part of humanity. I wished Rhys was there so I could point out, *See? I'm not becoming one of them.*

Corey led the way since people, including burly men, naturally stepped out of his path. We walked along the right side of the bar and found Kestrel near the back. She traced patterns in the droplets of water on the wooden surface. My nose told me that the amber liquid in the smaller of the two glasses in front of her was an expensive brand of Irish whiskey. Yes, I knew alcohol. Being a living substance, it didn't speak to me so much as it had its own faint energy. Not enough to keep me from consuming it, of course.

The other glass held ice water. I could tell which she'd been consuming more of.

"Are y'all here for her?" The pretty brunette bartender motioned toward Kestrel with the glass she was polishing.

"Yes," Corey replied. "How long has she been here?"

"Couple hours. I've been pacing her, but she's bad off." She cocked her head. "You don't look so hot yourself."

"Yes, ma'am. We're on our way to a funeral." Never mind that none of us wore black.

"Oh, poor thing. Right. I'll get the check."

She wandered off, and Corey sat beside Kestrel.

"Kes? Sweetie? Are you all right?"

She didn't appear all right. I raised both eyebrows, and Lawrence elbowed me.

Corey got the message and didn't wait for an answer. "What happened to you? Where've you been?"

"Nowhere." Kestrel didn't raise her head. "Everywhere. I needed to think." She placed her palms on the bar and pushed herself to an upright position, then looked at Corey with red-rimmed eyes. "I needed to find...myself." She buried her face in her hands.

Corey put an arm around her. "Your dad's been worried. We all have."

"Why? I'm an"—*hiccup*—"adult. I can do what I want."

Lawrence and I glanced at each other. We both knew she was twenty.

"Here you go, honey." The bartender laid a check presenter in front of Kestrel.

"Did you check her ID?" Lawrence asked.

"Yes, it's required by law." She took Corey's credit card and disappeared again.

"Kestrel, let me see it," Lawrence said.

"See what, Uncle Lawrence?" She giggled.

"Your fake ID."

"Don't have one. She saw my real one. But didn't see it. Guess my illusion powers have turned on again."

Of all the times for her to be having a magic flash...

I placed a finger on her forehead and drew energy from the stones around me. They had soaked up the energy from the fermented substances spilled in the building and the emotions of those going in and out of it for years and happily gave some of it up. Kestrel's eyes went out of focus as I made the alcohol in her bloodstream dissipate. Some of it had already metabolized, and if I'd had access to my full powers, I could have taken care of it, too, but as it was...

Kestrel's forehead went from clammy to hot, and I removed my finger. She blinked, then put a hand to her head. "Ow! What did you do to me?"

"Skipped you straight from drunk to hangover."

She glared at me. "That's no fun."

"Are you all right?" Corey asked. He grabbed the half-full glass of ice water and handed it to her. "Here, this will help."

"She'll be fine," I told him.

"Neat trick," Corey said with his usual half-amused expression. "I'll have to remember that."

I shook my hand, which tingled like I'd been sitting on it and it had just woken up. "It's not pleasant for either party, but it had to be done."

The bartender returned, and Corey signed the slip, put his card back in his wallet, and gestured for us to follow him. We did, weaving around the crowd at the front half of the bar. One young man started to approach Kestrel but stopped and backed off when Corey glared at him. Corey emanated power, and his aura sparked with protective energy. Whether either of them realized it or not, he'd chosen Kestrel for his mate.

That should be interesting. Whereas the lycanthropes had made peace with the Wizard Tribunal, and so werewolves and witches could mate, I didn't know where the Consolidated Were-Council—basically all the other non-elemental shifters —stood. Probably nowhere firm. They weren't that organized.

"What do you want?" Kestrel asked once we were outside and headed toward Corey's truck.

"Besides to make sure you're alive?" Corey growled. His chest heaved with a deep breath, and his already-golden eyes glowed. I almost reached out to him to help him get himself under control, but I waited. None of these creatures were my concern beyond the help I needed from them.

"I'm fine. Was fine." Kestrel shot me another irritated look. She hadn't stopped rubbing her head, and Corey fished a bottle of water from a cooler in the truck's flatbed.

"Here, this will help. Let me know if you need to throw up."

"Thanks."

The moment of peace between them only lasted until we got into the truck. Kestrel and I squeezed into the back, leaving the front for the taller men. I sat behind Corey, and I could see his face in the rearview mirror, so I braced myself.

"What were you thinking?" he asked. His voice, while not raised, thrummed with tension. "Don't you think your dad has been through enough these past few days? Don't you think we all have?"

She crossed her arms and pouted. "Don't *you* think I have? I deserve to blow off some steam."

Lawrence spoke and sounded every inch the concerned uncle. It was kind of cute. "Getting drunk isn't the answer, Kestrel. You could've gotten arrested for underage drinking."

She rolled her eyes, her sigh full of annoyance. "I'm not going to say anything that will get y'all off my back, am I?"

"Nope." Corey flexed one hand, then the other, and the white disappeared from his knuckles. "You need to call your dad and tell him you're sorry for scaring him."

She shook her head and leaned back. Now that her mind had cleared except for hangover pain, feelings crashed through her in waves so strong I didn't have to try too hard to see her aura. Sorrow, hurt, frustration, and anger rippled through her. The illusion power also made an appearance in flashes of smoky blue. Since she'd had trouble settling into any one type of witchy talent, I wondered if this would be hers. Or would it disappear as other powers had?

"Have you had Illusion before?" I asked to bring her attention out of her dark thoughts.

"Yeah, briefly." She rubbed her face and took another swig of water. "It didn't stick around this long."

"Can you feel it?"

"Yes. It feels like it's trying to stick, but something is keeping it from getting a foothold. Like I've got nonstick coating on my soul."

"That's interesting. Usually witches can't feel their powers separate from them."

"I'm aware of that, Doctor River." She shook her head. "That's what's wrong with me."

"Hmmm..." I tapped my lips with my index finger. Sir Raleigh took the opportunity to nudge his head under my hand. I placed that hand on the seat between me and Kestrel, and he jumped down and rubbed against her arm. She couldn't resist the invitation and scratched him on the head.

"He's growing fast. He's not a regular kitty, is he?"

"Nope. He's a grimalkin, a creature of the dark Fae." Well, gray Fae, really, but I didn't have authorization to speak of Fae politics to non-Fae.

She lifted her hand from his soft fur. "Is he dangerous?"

He half-rose on his hind legs to nudge her hand. "He doesn't think so." I smiled when he came to demand affection from me, and I complied and rubbed his ears, which he loved. "And would I be toting a dangerous creature around on my shoulder?"

Her green gaze met my own. "I honestly don't know. It's not like the Fae are known for being safe to talk to."

I laughed. "Touché."

Lawrence glanced back at us. "I texted John. He wants us to meet him at the house. Do you have any objection to going there first?"

"No." I wasn't going to say so in front of Kestrel, but I wanted to see what clues I could find to answer the question of why Cimex had shot Beverly Graves.

4

———

LAWRENCE

Watching Reine, Kestrel, and the cat—I mean, grimalkin—alleviated some of the pain around my heart. I had known the sting of grief, and one thing I hated about it was how every new experience brought up the old. I'd dreamed of my father's murder, the only other one I'd witnessed, the night before. It had hurt to wake alone from it, and I'd rushed to Stone Mountain to search for Reine. She'd healed me, and I suspected her strength had run low.

Why hadn't she asked me to take her to recharge?

That discussion would have to wait. Kestrel hurt. The fact, although obvious, bore stating again. How would she handle the compounding of betrayal, knowing her mother had taken extreme measures to make her daughter into something she wasn't? Most humans would shy away from such intense pain, but Reine, bless her Fae heart, jumped right into it, and the cat had coaxed a brief smile from my adopted niece with his antics. I'd started to think of him as an extension of Reine and her feelings, and who could say he wasn't? I'd have to keep studying him...and her.

The Graves' house appeared the same as it always had, but it felt like an invisible hole had been blasted through it. The energy of the place missed something vital—Beverly. I almost expected her to meet us at the door, wiping her hands on an apron or dish towel. She'd had that interesting ability—to present as completely domestic one minute and then as the powerful nature witch and administrative genius she was the next. I didn't know how John would get on without her.

He met us at the door, and he hugged Kestrel tightly before holding her away from him. "Where did you go?" he asked.

She turned her head, and he tilted her chin back up to him. None of us said anything. Instead, I waited for her to come clean about her stupid behavior like the adult she thought she was.

"I went somewhere to think." She smiled sadly.

"You smell like whiskey, but I don't sense any intoxication in your aura."

"Yeah, someone spilled some on me."

I didn't expect the disappointment to hit me like it did. I massaged the right side of my jaw so I could say, "We found her at a bar."

She turned to me with a glare. "Uncle Lawrence!"

"She was drunk," I continued. "Reine de-intoxicated her." A Fae ability I'd had no idea existed. Each day in her presence held a mix of frustration and discovery.

"That's...complex magic." John frowned briefly at the Fae, who shrugged. Then he turned his attention back to his daughter. "And you're grounded."

"Dad, I'm twenty. That's too old to be grounded."

"Then start acting like it." He turned and gestured for us to follow him into the house. We did, and Kestrel stomped up the stairs.

We walked through the living room, which was decorated

in earth tones as befit two nature witches. Whereas before it had felt cozy, now the atmosphere spoke more of underground tombs and burial sites. Reine briefly pinched her nose, and I wanted to ask her what she smelled. Earth? Blood, although the murder had taken place at the lab?

"How are you doing, Doctor Graves?" Corey asked. His reaction to Kestrel's grounding had been a flicker of disappointment, but otherwise his expression had remained concerned.

"Better now that you found Kestrel and brought her home. I don't know what she was thinking."

Reine surprised me by saying, "Don't be too hard on the girl. She's had two major shocks. Plus, her magic is acting up. That's probably why she wasn't upfront with you just now. She's under the influence, but not of a substance."

The line between John's brows deepened. "What do you mean? Wait, hold that. Where are my manners? Would you like something? I have coffee on."

She opened her mouth, then glanced at me, and I dipped my chin slightly to say yes. John found solace in domestic routines. He'd be more likely to be comfortable if he thought we were, so while I hated to delay, this was important, too.

Once we all sat with warm mugs of coffee—tea for Reine—John asked again, "What do you mean, Kestrel is under the influence of magic?"

"It's an interesting case," Reine said. "She's currently experiencing a flash of deception magic, which I think you call illusion magic here. Let me ask this—do you feel your nature magic as separate from you?"

John almost laughed. "No, it's as much a part of me as my body. You may as well ask if I feel my internal organs."

"Right, that's not how it is for her. Something is keeping the magic from integrating into her. With your permission, I'd like for her to accompany us so I can keep an eye on her."

"Is that safe?" I asked. "We're dealing with a soul-eater. What if it goes after her?"

"It's interested in me, not in her," Reine argued. "Kestrel's familiar with the convention. She's our chance to talk to the organizers, and even if they don't agree to shutter it, to help us convince them to alert us about anything strange."

"But it's still dangerous," Corey insisted. I hoped John appreciated Corey's protectiveness of his daughter. For some reason, John and Beverly hadn't approved of Corey's and Kestrel's relationship. Well, not for some reason, the obvious one. Kestrel was twenty—Corey in his late twenties. Plus, Corey had a dangerous career as an investigator for the PBI—Paranormal Bureau of Investigation.

"It's after me, not her," Reine replied. She sounded convinced, but I wasn't so sure. Plus, since Reine's brother had arrived, I'd seen more of the ruthless Fae poking through.

I spoke quietly so Kestrel wouldn't overhear. "John, you know you're not going to be able to contain Kestrel. Not right now in her current state. You have too much going on to watch her, and she'll be out of here as soon as you leave."

John ran his hands over his face. "You're right. I need someone to watch her who can monitor her current magic surge."

"I can't stay here," Reine said. "Not right now."

"And I've got my duties," Corey added.

John sighed, and I hated that his air of defeat deepened. "Fine, she can go with you. As long as you're there, too, Lawrence."

"I will be." I didn't say it, but I needed to watch Reine watching Kestrel. Fae had their own priorities.

John's phone rang, and he glanced at it, then snatched it up. "Be right back." He walked into the living room.

"All right, then," Reine said. "I'll babysit Kestrel...and Rhys."

"Who?" Corey asked. His eyes flared gold like they had at the bar. It seemed we all were slipping in control over our magic. I'd felt my inner gargoyle wanting to come out in the stupid hotel manager's office, and it had been harder to resist the urge to scare the odious little man into wetting his pants.

"My brother." Reine massaged her temples. "He appeared this morning. My mother sent him to *help*."

"And so, he's what, a couple hundred years old?" Corey asked, no doubt picturing some old, gnarled male Fae.

"He's three hundred. Younger than me." She looked at him in an apparent challenge to judge her as old. Other than her silvery-white hair, she seemed to be in her twenties.

"Right. Lawrence, you'll keep an eye on her, too, right?" Corey asked.

"I already said I would."

John returned to the kitchen before the discussion could go further. "That was our toxicology lab. I knew everyone was acting erratically last night, so I had the rest of the open wine sent to be tested."

"You weren't," I pointed out.

"No, but I wasn't drinking. I knew I'd be too tired to drive home if I did."

"What did the lab find?"

"Some sort of foreign substance. They're still working on a match."

WITH A SULKY KESTREL IN TOW, we picked up my car at the crystal shop. Corey declined to join us for lunch, saying he'd been called back to the lab to aid in the investigation. Reine, Kestrel, and I grabbed a quick lunch, and returned to the Crowne Plaza Perimeter. Whereas in the morning the cars had been unloading mostly large equipment boxes with a smattering of arriving 'Con-goers, now they spewed forth giggling young men and women and older ones with indulgent smiles. Old friends greeted each other with hugs, and porters dragged luggage racks piled high with sparkling costumes and wings behind chatting cosplayers who already wore pointed ears.

One young brunette in a blue dress and fake wings said to Reine, "Oh, your ears are awesome!"

"Thanks, I've been working on them a long time."

"Nice job. Got any tips?"

"Just be yourself," Reine told her with a smirk. The girl's face fell into a disappointed expression, and she turned to join her friends.

"'Be yourself,' really?" Kestrel asked.

"Not sure what else to say." Reine shrugged. "Where do you think your friends who organize the convention are?"

"Probably at the main registration table. Come on, it's always in the same place."

"Right, hold on." Reine walked behind a pillar, and when she emerged, she no longer had the cat. "I don't want to antagonize the charming Jimmy Leak more than necessary. Sir Raleigh is hanging out in our room for now."

"Good call," I said, although I hadn't realized how accustomed I'd gotten to her having the gray kitten—now a young cat—draped across her shoulders. Not that she seemed naked, or that I needed the distraction of thinking of Reine and "naked" in the same sentence, but almost like she missed something. Was I growing attached to the silly critter?

We followed Kestrel through the lobby. The atmosphere held the buoyancy of escape, make-believe, and the fact that no matter who these people were in their everyday lives, here they could be part of a group of kindred spirits and accepted for who they were. I'd felt something similar before, back when my gargoyle clan would gather for athletic contests, drinking spir-its, and catching up. That hadn't happened since my father's murder, which had been the start of a persecution. Now I didn't know where my family members were or if they still lived. I thought I'd found a new family with the Graves and my CPDC colleagues, but that had been shattered, too.

Knowing I could pick them up again any time, I released the sad memories and tried to take in the giddiness. As per usual, I felt more like I observed others' happiness rather than experiencing it for myself. And then there was the predator in their midst. In truth, probably some of the human sort lurked about, too, to take advantage of careless 'Con-goers. My inner gargoyle stirred at the angry turn of my thoughts, and to calm it, I shifted my attention to Kestrel, who seemed to relax into her skin as she greeted old friends. Did the events of the past few days seem more like a nightmare for her while here in these familiar and comforting surroundings? I suspected the murder receded a smidgen, but the shadow still loomed.

Rhys found us just as we approached the main registration desk. "Where have you been?" he asked. "I'm starving."

Something about his voice made me want to garg out on him, but I suppressed it.

"Get some food at the hotel restaurant," Reine told him. "It's not bad."

"Fine. Who's this?" He turned his crooked smile on Kestrel, who blushed like a redhead.

"I'm Kestrel."

"She's helping us," Reine said with a frown that said—*Don't even think about it.* "Kestrel, this is my brother Rhys. My mother sent him to help as well."

"Charmed to be on the same team as such a beauty." Rhys took the hand Kestrel had proffered to shake and kissed the back of it. Her face went an even deeper shade of red.

"And that's enough." I took Kestrel's hand back from his and squeezed it. She blinked, coming out of whatever spell Rhys had tried on her. Forget going full-gargoyle on him, I wanted to punch him in the mouth. Hard. It would be faster.

"Right, go get food," Reine said. "We'll meet you back here shortly. Kestrel?"

"I'm okay," she replied, too quickly. At least her skin returned to its normal paleness with a light smattering of freckles across her cheekbones.

"Whatever you say, sis." With a nod to us, Rhys stalked across the lobby. He moved like a panther, and several of the women in the space turned their heads to watch him before he disappeared down the stairs to the cafe level.

"Watch out for Fae," I told Kestrel. "You can't trust them."

Reine stiffened but didn't say anything. She arched an eyebrow and inclined her head toward a sign pointing us to registration. "We have things to do."

"I didn't mean you." I jogged to catch up with her fast, angry steps.

"Well, what did you mean?"

"All the Fae but you. You know as well as I do that they're tricky. Like, are you sure your brother is here to help? He hasn't exactly done anything useful."

"We don't know that. He could have been gathering information. I'll ask him later."

Of course, she'd defend him.

We approached the main registration, and a large, heavyset guy with bronze skin and black hair and beard grinned when he saw Kestrel.

"There's my girl," he said. "I didn't think you were coming this year."

"Samir, these are my friends, Reine and Lawrence. Y'all, this is Samir. He's one of the 'Con's organizers."

"Awesome ears, Lady Reine." He bowed. "What can I do for you?"

"Do you have a moment to speak privately?" Reine smiled, and his eyes went fuzzy for a second. Was she trying to manipulate him with a glamour? I'd seen her do it before with Robert Cannon, but it wasn't necessary here. I crossed my arms over the itch of the irritation in my chest.

"Anything for you, Madame." He walked around the tables to come to our side. "Follow me."

"Does he know who she is?" Kestrel whispered to me.

"I don't know. He seems to sense something special about her." Which didn't help my annoyance.

"And do you?" She glanced up at me coyly.

"None of your business, dearie."

She snickered. "Yeah, you do."

We stepped into a ballroom that had been set up with row upon row of chairs, all facing a raised stage with a large screen behind it. No one was in there...yet.

"What can I do for you?" Samir asked. He put his hands in his pockets.

"You need to call off the 'Con," Reine told him with uncharacteristic directness for a Fae.

Samir's eyes widened. "What do you mean? Why?"

"There's a predator on the loose, a soul-eater. It gains energy by taking over people and stealing their spiritual life force. Some have died. Others are in comas. You recall that young woman who fainted earlier?"

Samir nodded. "I'd heard about something, but that always happens at these things. That's why I hire an emergency medical team."

"She'd been taken over briefly so the creature could give me a message."

Samir put a hand to his forehead. "Oh, I know what this is.

This is a role-playing adventure thing, isn't it? Invisible Monster Stalking the 'Con."

"No, it's real," Kestrel said. "I saw its work last night."

"Kes, that's incredible." He looked back at us. "This girl doesn't break character. You know I'll do anything for you, but I can't cancel the 'Con for a roleplay, no matter how realistic. The Fae Princess is a nice touch—I need to get prosthetics lessons from you after this is over because those ears...damn."

Reine had been careful to hide her ears until the 'Con. Rhys had never bothered. Did he come from an area populated by supernatural creatures who didn't have to hide from humans? Or did he just not care? I suspected the latter. It fit his personality.

"Samir, please," Kestrel begged. "We're not role-playing. People could get hurt or killed."

"Fine. You bring me evidence, and I'll reconsider. Oh!" He held up an index finger, then pointed at me and Reine. "What did you say your last names are?"

"I'm Doctor Lawrence Gordon, and this is Doctor Renee River."

Our titles did not seem to impress him, but Samir did say, "Right, Jimmy Leak mentioned something to me about giving a couple of people access to backstage areas. I thought your names sounded familiar. Sure, I'll hook you up with VIP guest passes. Then you can get access to all the 'Con rooms and Green Room, and I'll tell my staff to let you into their restricted areas as well." He shrugged. "That's all I can do right now."

"Does that mean you believe me?" Kestrel gave him the hopeful smile that had melted many men, including Corey. Sometimes.

"I don't know if I do. But I'll help."

"All right, thanks," Reine told him. "Could I get one more pass for my brother?"

"Sure, Princess, whatever you ask." Samir bowed. "Meanwhile, I gotta get back. Stuff always comes up during setup."

He walked out of the room, and Kestrel followed him. Reine paused when she got to the ballroom door.

"What is it?" I asked.

She reached to her shoulder, then clenched her fist, presumably realizing the cat wasn't there. "The soul-eater is here."

5

REINE

When I walked out of the ballroom, the air moved past me in a rush that made no sense according to the laws of hotel HVAC physics, but did indicate my foe had taken its invisible form and was stalking me.

"What is it?" Lawrence asked.

"The soul-eater is here." I reached for Sir Raleigh, then bit back a groan of frustration. Right, he couldn't be with me in public spaces, so I'd sent him away. He'd hesitated, but then seemed to understand the need to do so after I reminded him we could all get kicked out of the 'Con.

Lawrence glanced around, and his eyes went black. I placed my hand on his forearm. "No, don't change here."

He closed his eyes, his brows drawn together and his jaw clenched. "It's hard to control today. Since this morning."

"It makes sense. Your threat alert is up, for good reason."

He nodded and opened his eyes, which had returned to their usual slate gray.

"Do you know where it is now?"

"No." Sir Raleigh appeared on my shoulder. He vibrated with a low growl. "But it's still close."

I did my best to hide the cat with my hair, and we followed Samir and Kestrel to the registration desk. He handed me two badges, Lawrence one.

"Where'd the cat come from?" he asked.

"It's a long story. Thanks for the badges."

"Cool, you can have Kitty with you as long as you have documentation that it's an emotional support animal. Georgia law doesn't say we have to allow them, but the 'Con does, and it's in our agreement with the hotel."

Emotional support animal? What in Hades was that? "Um, I don't have any paperwork with me, but I'll get it." Perhaps I could get Selene to write up something for me. She was a psychologist, after all.

Samir looked around. "Better carry the letter with you. The hotel manager's kind of a dick."

"I'd noticed."

"Also, if it's not friendly, I can't say that will be enough."

I'd tuned Sir Raleigh's low growl out, but I could feel his vibrations and see his poufy tail in my peripheral vision. He was likely in full Halloween cat arch, or as much as he could be on my shoulders. "You'd asked for proof of what we were talking about. Sir Raleigh here can sense it."

Samir shrugged. "Sorry, still not proof enough. Cats are temperamental. He could be reacting to being around too many people."

I sighed and put Rhys' badge in my back pocket. I clipped the other one to the lapel of my faux leather jacket. The badge had a picture of a cute little pixie on a purple background and VIP in big letters on a sticker across the bottom.

"Well, thanks again." I turned and walked away, and Lawrence hurried after me.

"Are you okay?"

I brushed a hand over Sir Raleigh's soft, bristling fur. "Sir Raleigh is getting to me. He doesn't want me here, but if the soul-eater is around, I don't feel comfortable just leaving it to wreak its havoc. What if it hurts someone else?"

"And what will you do if you find it?"

"Good question." It's not like I had a brilliant plan for capturing or killing it, but I wasn't going to say that out loud.

Information, I needed information...

The opening ceremonies were on the cusp of starting, and Lawrence and I walked through the sparse crowd of 'Con-goers who were heading into the large ballroom. I studied each one for signs of possession. I also kept one hand on Sir Raleigh, whose grumbling had subsided, but whose tension came through in the grip of his paws and claws—*ouch*—and the arch of his back. I'd not experienced anxiety about the unseen like this since a brief outbreak of typhoid fever in Lycan Village in the early 1800s. It had taken people quickly, but some had been carriers who never showed symptoms, and for a while, everyone had regarded their neighbor with suspicion. I'd done some major glamouring and manipulation to keep the local healing woman from being burned as a witch.

I shook my head to clear the memory and the feelings of isolation and overwhelming responsibility that came with it. Not that those were unfamiliar...

Where had Rhys gone, and what sort of mess would I have to clean up when he found me again?

"Hey! You, with the awesome ears."

I turned toward the voice and saw the young woman who had fainted.

"Hello." I gave her my friendliest smile. "How are you feeling?"

She didn't smile back. "Weird. What happened to me? I know that sleazy hotel manager is lying."

"What do you mean?" Lawrence asked.

"I've never had anything like that happen to me before. It

was weird. And scary." She glared, but her eyes sparkled with tears.

I drew her aside to a quiet corner of the hall, and Lawrence followed. Sir Raleigh leaned down from my shoulder, his paws on my left breast, and asked, "Mrrowr?"

"Awww." The young woman immediately softened and scratched him behind the ears. Her name badge said she went by Lady Sparkle—yes, I refrained from rolling my eyes, but barely. "Is this your kitty?"

"Yes, this is Sir Raleigh. He's an, uh, emotional support animal."

She drew her hand back and sneezed. "Sorry, allergic. But he's just too cute."

"Yes, he is." Being a Fae creature, he'd likely done some of his own glamouring to make her pet him and calm her down. He passed some interesting info on to me—she'd been shaken to her core by the experience, which she recognized as paranormal.

"Can we talk?" she asked. Her confrontational demeanor had dissipated, leaving a scared young woman.

"Yes, of course."

Kestrel joined us, and she and Lady Sparkle studied each other for a second, then shrieked and hugged each other.

"Kestrel! I didn't think you were going to be here." Sparkle, well, almost sparkled with delight, and her aura flared with newly charged earth energy.

I studied her and mentally removed the heavy eye shadow, glittery sheen, and rainbow streaks in her hair and saw a familiar face. She'd been at the Equinox ceremony Kestrel's parents' coven had hosted the day before. Had it only been the previous morning? It felt like a week ago. The Fae definitely didn't have the monopoly on screwing with time perception. They shared it with tragedy.

"I didn't think I'd attend Fae-Con this year, either." The

shadow of the last twenty-four hours flitted across Kestrel's face. "I have some bad news." She stopped, took a deep breath, and pressed her lips together. Then she shook her head and turned to the side, her fist to her mouth.

"Her mother is dead," Lawrence said gently and put a hand on Kestrel's shoulder. She allowed him to draw her to his side. I sensed this was the first time she'd allowed herself to cry since she'd left the lab, and I was glad she and Lawrence had a good uncle-niece relationship.

"Oh!" Sparkle's eyes and mouth made the same round dismayed shapes, and she hugged her friend. "I'm so, so sorry! Then why are you here?"

I answered for Kestrel, who tried unsuccessfully to speak through the sobs that came from her gut.

"It has to do with what happened to you this morning, but I don't want to talk about it in public."

"Ooookay." But she didn't argue.

I led our little group out of the gathering area past the authors' and organizations' tables and dodged the hopeful greetings of the people hoping I'd buy something or make a donation. I promised myself I'd reward myself with a good book once all this was over. It would be a last gift to myself before returning to Faerie.

Rhys joined us in the lobby. He carried a brown paper bag and two paper cups, one of which he handed to me. "Tea for you, sis."

"Thank you." I traded his badge for a cup of tea. His kind gesture almost made me cry, and I recognized just how strained my nerves had become. I still examined each person we passed, and the thoughts darted through my brain. Had that young man's smile been too wide? Had that chick just given me a strange look? The dude who had just yawned and glanced sideways at me, had his lips formed a leer or a threat before he'd closed his mouth? And in every conversation we overheard as we walked by, the sounds floated out and formed the echoes of, "I'll get you, I'll get you, I'll get you..."

Lawrence's hand on my upper back alerted me to the fact I'd hunched my shoulders against all of it, and I forced my muscles to release. Ending up with a Fae of a headache wouldn't help anything.

We took the elevators up to my and Lawrence's rooms. The wards had faded, so I reinforced them while Lawrence brought Kestrel to the armchair in my room and poured her a Coke from the stash he'd apparently bought that morning. I wouldn't touch the stuff, but I understood some humans found the fizzy brown chemical and sugar concoction to be soothing.

I sipped my tea as Kestrel explained to her friend what had happened. The night before, a staff happy hour at her parents' lab had gone very wrong and her mother had been killed by the head of the lab. She glossed over her getting drunk and me getting her un-drunk, and told Sparkle about the soul-eater and attempting to get the 'Con shut down. Other than her omissions, she gave a very good summary. I could see her PBI training in evidence and hoped she'd be able to continue her education and join Corey on the force in spite of all of this.

She finished with, "But no one believes us."

I started to form a question, but Rhys beat me to it. He gave Sparkle—I really needed to learn her real name—a charming smile and asked, "What did it feel like when the soul-eater possessed you, love? Since you're a witch, you may have noticed something an ordinary human wouldn't."

She preened under the compliment and charm for a second, then shuddered. "Slimy. Like something invisible was trying to get inside me and drive. Which it did. I couldn't fight it, but then with a flash of light, it left."

"What color light?" I asked.

She frowned. "Blue, I think. Then yellow. Then everything went dark."

Rhys, who had been sitting on the bed and eating a sandwich, raised his eyebrows at me. *Slimy* sounded very much like the dark Fae. Not that they were, but that's how humans and light Fae perceived their energy and why they were so hard to catch. Slippery and gross. If they came with visual sensations, it was often a flash of what people called UV light or black light. Or a certain shade of puce or something like it.

The blue flash of light, on the other hand...

Ugh, this information confirmed that the soul-eater had indeed been released in a collaboration between a light and dark Fae, and not just any light Fae. The contributor of the light energy had come from the capital of the realm. The other cities had their own colors, and energy from a countryside Fae would have been green. The question was, who had it been? My mother wouldn't be any help. Could I try to contact my grandmother? No, I didn't have the energy to do it even when I'd been in Scotland and at my full strength. I'd have to wait for her to reach out to me again, if she could.

Meanwhile, I'd also need to figure out how to capture the soul-eater and question it, not just banish it.

"What are you thinking?" Lawrence asked. He'd retreated back into his stony expression, and I guessed he'd seen Rhys' and my looks and felt excluded.

"We need to capture the soul-eater," I said. "Question it. Find out what it wants and who sent it, light and dark Fae because both are involved, and then bring that knowledge to my grandmother. Otherwise, we're only going to have to deal with more creatures, which they'll send after me until they succeed."

"Who's your grandmother, again?" Kestrel asked.

Oh, right, there were humans present. Not that it mattered. Kestrel had already heard about my royal lineage, although not in detail.

"Tatiana, also known as the Queen of Faerie."

Sparkle curtsied low to me. "Your majesty."

"Please don't do that," I told her. "I'm not even close to the throne, and I'm in exile. No royal trappings here, just an unlucky Fae." I couldn't resist a side-eye at Rhys for that, then I immediately felt guilty. He'd been the one to be maimed and therefore had no chance of being allowed back in to the Fae realm, which only accepted the perfect.

"But this is Fae-Con," Sparkle argued. "And you are a Fae princess. I believe you need to work that in order to gain allies in your fight against this creature."

Rhys snorted. "She's thinking more like a Fae than you are, sis."

They both had a point. I needed to gather allies and consider the ones I already had. "Should I start addressing you as General Sparkle?" I asked.

She saluted. "I'll spread the word that if anything strange happens, it needs to be reported to me or Kestrel."

"Yes." Kestrel drew her mouth into a grim line. "I want to help take this thing down."

"Fine, but be careful. We know it's after me, and if it knows you're helping me, it may attack you."

Sir Raleigh jumped down from my shoulder to the bed and engaged in a vigorous session of face-cleaning. Two whiskers dropped from his face and lay in tapered black lines on the teal bedspread. Then he meowed at me as if to say, "Don't just stand there, Dummy. You know what to do with these."

"Oh, right. Clever kitty." I handed a whisker to each girl. "Sir Raleigh can tell when the creature is near. Even if he's not with you, this will vibrate if it gets close, and all you have to do is whisper Sir Raleigh's name. He'll come aid you." Not that I knew what he'd do, but he could be impressive when threatened.

"What are you going to do?" Rhys asked.

I checked my watch. "Lawrence, can you make a date for us

to have an interview with a vampire?" Not that I wanted to be in debt to someone like Ashlee Wyatt, but she was our only other ally with supernatural power in this situation.

"I'll see what I can do." Lawrence cocked his head at Rhys. "What about him?"

Rhys brushed crumbs from his hands and grinned at the two young women. "I'll help out downstairs."

"Please don't make any trouble," I said.

"You can trust me, sis."

But could I? Apparently, I had no choice.

KESTREL FOLLOWED THE OTHERS OUT, then turned around in the hallway. I tried to ignore her, although I acknowledged my annoyance was irrational.

"What?" I finally asked. She stepped forward, then paused at the door, waiting to be invited in.

"I need your help," she said. "If I'm going to help you, that is."

"How so?" I stepped back for her to enter and watched to see if she reacted at all to the wards. I'd forgotten to observe when she'd entered the first time. She shivered, which I took as a good sign. She could at least sense magic. The door closed behind her with a determined click.

"I need you to help me find my true powers. Ones that will stick." The determination in her expression reminded me of the first night we'd talked via magical video chat. "I'll give you whatever you like. Even my firstborn."

A laugh bubbled up from a deep place inside me, and although I put my hand over my mouth, I couldn't stop it. Dear gods, she reminded me of so many humans before her asking me to do the impossible and offering things I neither wanted nor needed.

"Have you checked this with Corey?" I asked, unable to resist teasing her. The deep shade she blushed made it worth it, and I laughed harder.

"What? No! Why do you keep laughing?"

"Because I haven't been in the baby trading business for several hundred years." The mirth left me, and I plopped on the bed, feeling hollow. "And changelings were never my thing."

"Oh, so what do you want?"

Now guilt crept in. I'd definitely acted the Fae bitch. "Nothing. Your and Sparkle's help are enough. Come here." I patted the bed beside me.

She approached cautiously, and I couldn't blame her. Yep, my Fae side had definitely come out. Kestrel sat about three feet away from me and regarded me warily.

"I need to know what my true power is," she said. "Or powers. This trying on different ones is exhausting, especially since I can't control when they come and go." She didn't add what I'm sure we were both thinking—that if her powers had settled earlier, her mother might not have taken the desperate action she had and might still be alive.

All right, I felt truly rotten now for mocking her. Interacting with Rhys definitely brought out the worst in me, or at least the Fae in me.

"Have any of them stuck around longer than others?" I asked. "Even for just a few hours?"

She shook her head and brought out her phone. "I started tracking them. My mother suggested I do that so I could see what direction I may be moving." She closed her eyes and swiped her hands across her cheeks.

Gods. I scooted closer to her and put my arm around her slowly to give her the chance to move away. She didn't. She leaned over, put her arms around me, and sobbed into my shoulder. Sir Raleigh curled up against her opposite hip, and he purred so loudly that the air in the room seemed to vibrate with it.

When her sobbing subsided and she straightened, I got up and grabbed the tissue box from the bathroom.

"Here," I said and presented her with the box. "How are you feeling?"

"Rotten." She sniffled and took a tissue, then wiped her eyes and blew her nose noisily. I refrained from complimenting her on being a pretty crier. Most women would have puffy faces, but in her case, a slight flush illuminated her cheekbones, and her glistening eyes gave her an innocent air.

Yes, I am a *shallow,* bitchy Fae.

"That's to be expected." I sat beside her, but with a foot between us again. "Thank you for trusting me with your grief." And her tears. They still soaked my shirt, and the emotion plus the water felt like fizz against my skin, but in an invigorating way. Yes, water plus salt plus spirit was like a drug to some Fae, hence why they loved making humans suffer. For me, the pleasant sensation recharged parts of me, but not in a way that made me addicted to it.

She blew her nose again with a honk, and I made a note to tell her later that she might want to work on that very unladylike sound. "You're welcome, I guess? I still want you to help me."

"Right. How strong is the deception power right now? It may keep me from doing what I need."

"At about an eight out of ten." Another sniffle. "Mom had me rate their strengths, too."

"Your sorrow may help me get past it."

"I definitely feel like I'm cracked down the middle." She sighed. "What do you need to do?"

"I need to peek inside you and see if I can tell what's going on. Don't worry, it shouldn't hurt."

The way her brows drew together showed her skepticism

about the amount of pain she might experience, but she nodded. "I'll do anything."

"Be careful with your words, Kestrel. Most Fae will not be as kind or ethical as I am."

"Noted." She closed her eyes. "I'm ready."

I recalled doing the same with Lawrence after his poisoning had become evident, and I wished he could be there with me, although he might not approve of me scanning his niece.

"Hold still." I moved closer to her and put my fingers on her temples. Her skin felt hot under my touch, the burning of emotion and pain. Her internal fire allowed me to get past the layer of the deception magic that covered her, just inside her skin. Grief engulfed her, and I recognized the determination that made us kindred spirits—no matter what she went through, she would strive to accomplish what she felt she needed, and her inability to manifest a power type consistently frustrated her. If she could, then maybe she could use it to help her win her father over to Corey since she'd be better able to take care of herself.

I tried to move away from the private thoughts and feelings, especially those having to do with me. If I wasn't careful, she'd attach to me as her dominant female guardian, and I didn't need a dependent, especially not a twenty-year-old witch who couldn't figure out her magic.

When I started the scan, I'd made a rookie mistake—I hadn't set the intention for what I needed or hoped to find. As a physician, I needed to run the right tests to figure out the answers to what ailed a patient. She'd described the issue as her powers staying separate from her rather than being part of her that emerged. I realigned my intention to what I hoped to accomplish—find out what blocked her and kept the powers from sticking. I searched for some spell, then when that turned up empty, some sort of psychic block coming from her. Nothing made itself evident. She desperately wished for her powers to manifest, and it frustrated her that they didn't, but she wasn't blocking them.

Finally, with a frustrated sigh, I pulled out and rubbed her temples in a widdershins direction to release her.

When she opened her eyes, their blue irises practically radiated hope. "What did you find?"

"Nothing."

The black of shock, then red of frustration popped in her aura, making it briefly visible. "Nothing?"

"Nothing. There's no spell keeping you from manifesting your powers, and there's no psychic block, either. I don't know why they won't stick."

I braced myself for her reaction. Would there be more tears? They wouldn't be pleasant to me if they were connected to a failure.

"I see," she said quietly and folded her hands in her lap. "Well, thanks for trying."

"That's it?" I asked.

She shrugged and looked up at me with a resigned twist to her mouth. "If you'd found something less than twenty-four hours after my mother's death, I might have felt worse. Like if only I'd asked you to do this sooner, we could have prevented everything. Or maybe not. But I would have always wondered."

Her disappointment seeped from her, and I had to acknowledge her strangely mature response.

"I'm sorry," I said, although I didn't know what I apologized for. Fae didn't do sorry, but healers did, especially those who had failed. Both apology and failure were novel and unpleasant experiences for me.

"That's all right. I guess." She stood. "I should go, use the remains of this deception power for some good. I'll let you know what, if anything, I find."

"Thanks." I preceded her to the door and opened it. Another apology wanted to come out, but I bit my tongue over it. Once she left, I quickly closed the door behind her before anything unwanted could try to get in.

"What did you see?" I asked Sir Raleigh, who had remained close to her the whole time. He turned around and curled up to take a nap. "Thanks, some help you are. I'll add this puzzle to the growing pile."

What would Lawrence think about me probing his niece with my own powers? She'd asked me, but considering his reaction to Fae in general, he might not appreciate it.

Right, me and Lawrence. Besides the soul-eater, that was the biggest conundrum of them all, topped by, why did I care so much what he thought?

6

LAWRENCE

Ted insisted on meeting me alone without Reine before he'd agree to set up another meeting between us and the vampire night club co-owner Ashlee Wyatt. I'd hated to leave Reine alone, but she said she needed to rest. What she didn't say—she needed to stay at the hotel to make sure Rhys didn't cause too much trouble. Plus, she wanted to be available in case one of the girls needed help. They and Rhys would circulate through the 'Con and gather information.

I suspected the attacks by the soul-eater had taken more out of her than she let on, so I supported her desire to conserve her strength, as long as she did, indeed, stay in the room and rest. I hoped the soul-eater wouldn't be active without Reine in attendance, but it could surprise us. Fae, whether light or dark, did have a reputation for capriciousness. If it acted outside of stalking Reine, the soul-eater could provide a clue to its overall agenda and perhaps point to a way to capture it.

A flimsy plan, yes, but what else did we have?

I drove to Ted's house through the spring afternoon that would have been beautiful had it not been for the dark undercurrent of my thoughts. Also, every mile away from Reine made my jaw clench with the effort not to turn into my gargoyle self, drive back to the hotel, and claim her.

Protect her, I sternly told that spot in my chest that wanted to explode into fierceness and power. *Not claim her.* Not that I hadn't enjoyed the kiss we'd shared or the feeling of her curled against me the previous night. She'd been the anchor in the emotional turmoil of Beverly's death and Lucius Cimex's betrayal.

Seeing Reine and Rhys question Lady Sparkle made me wonder if it would be useful to do the same with Lucius. Lucius had acted so out of character. I knew in my gut he would *never* have hurt any of us, especially not Beverly. No, he'd been manipulated somehow. Perhaps the toxicology results of the analysis of the wine would reveal something, but I didn't know what.

I'd always known office happy hours were a bad idea.

Ted met me at the door before I could even knock. Red rimmed his eyes, which also sported dark bags under them, and his cheeks simultaneously appeared hollow and flaccid. In short, he seemed long on stress and short on sleep. I supposed I did, too, because he looked me up and down, then motioned for me to follow him inside. He lived in a large, gray brick house in a neighborhood known for poshness and flooding. His choice of domicile had surprised me, considering his wizardly talent was prognostication. I supposed he liked the risk and being able to warn his neighbors when Battle Creek tried to become Battle Lake, then Battle Swamp. Maybe he felt helping his neighbors prepare for when things would get bad helped him not feel guilty about the advantage his prediction power gave him in the journalistic world, where he was a reporter known for his strange ability to be in the right place at the right time to grab scoops for a popular local news show.

He led me through his living room, which was decorated in

bachelor chic with lots of leather and a large television—he owned several—and out to his back deck, where he'd set up his outside bar.

"Here." He handed me a squat cubic glass of amber-colored liquid. A perfectly clear spherical ice cube floated in it and clinked musically against the sides. He'd finished the cocktail with a curl of orange peel.

I sniffed—earthy, herbal, smoky, fruity... "What is it?"

"Old-fashioned. Like you."

"Ted, it's two o'clock! Isn't it early to be playing bartender?"

He picked up an identical drink and tapped my glass with his. "Cheers!" He took a long swallow. His bloodshot eyes told me it hadn't been his first.

I turned toward the back lawn and took a careful sip. The drink burned going down, but in a good way. The grass behind the house sloped down to a retaining wall, below which the infamous Battle Creek flowed among trees and various shade plants. As a creature of water and earth, I found the stream and its rocky red clay bed more soothing than the drink. I knew I'd have to drive back to the hotel, and I'd sip at the cocktail if it was in my hand, so I placed the Old Fashioned on a coaster on a small table.

Ted motioned me to sit in one of the chairs beside the table, and we settled in and gazed out over the peaceful scene.

I decided to try a different question. "What's the occasion?" Then, his behavior and his talent clicked in my overtired and overwrought brain. "You have bad news for me."

"Go ahead and drink," he said. "We both know it takes at least three of those to impair you. I'm trying to take the edge off."

"This isn't good." My churning stomach warned me that if I tried to drink anymore, I'd regret it. "If you have something for me, please spit it out. I can't take the suspense. Not after everything that's happened."

He shook his head and leaned forward, his elbows on his knees. "I can't make sense of it until I have context. Why did you call me today?"

I knew the paranormal authorities would have kept the news of last night's murder out of the press, so I filled him in on what had happened and finished with, "And we think it has something to do with the creature that threatened Reine and killed the bouncer outside of the vampire club. Ashlee had offered to help us capture it, so we were hoping to meet with her, tonight if possible."

"And you need my help with that why?"

"We didn't exactly leave on good terms with her general manager—what's his name, Rae? He basically threatened Reine." I took another cautious sip in case he was getting offended at my not drinking. "So, can you help us?"

"I assume the *us* is you and the Fae, not the royal *we*."

"Yes, obviously."

He flopped back in his chair and covered his face with his hands for a breath, then dropped them and asked, "What's going on with you two?"

My turn to lean forward and study the scenery. "Nothing. And everything."

"What do you mean?"

"We kissed yesterday. It was..." I struggled to find the words. My brain didn't do emotions. They'd been banished from it, or at least locked way on a dark, dusty shelf in my psyche, long ago.

"Magical?" Ted asked.

I straightened and glared at him. "Gods, Ted, I'm not fourteen."

He smiled for the first time since I'd arrived. "No, you're four hundred, or something like that, and you've kissed a woman, what, three times?"

"Something like that." That was one area I'd never talked to him about much. Gargoyles didn't kiss—or sex—and tell. Not that I had a lot of experience regardless.

"Then what happened?"

"I saw one of my colleagues murdered in front of me. Reine comforted me last night." And had promised to not keep any more secrets, but she was Fae. I knew better, although something in me desperately wanted to trust her.

"Comforted how?" His expression turned curious.

"Not like you're thinking. We spent the night together fully clothed." And had held each other as the feelings crashed around me until I finally subsided into a fitful sleep. "And then when I woke, she'd left."

"Without saying goodbye or where she was going?"

"Yep." That still stung.

"She's Fae. She probably had her reasons. And where are things with the two of you now?"

I rubbed my chest, where the place the change started from still burned. "I want to protect her. Claim her..." *Kiss her some more, make love to her...* "Gargoyles used to be the traditional protectors of the Fae. I think that instinct has gotten activated."

"Which would be fascinating and worthy of study if it wasn't happening to you." He chuckled. "Sure, it's only instinct."

"You're right, and I don't know what to do if it's not."

His expression sobered, and he placed his right hand on my left forearm, a surprisingly intimate gesture from him. "Don't. Do. Anything."

"Wait, what do you mean?"

"That's what I saw. If you continue on your current course with the Fae, you'll have the answer to an old puzzle, but you'll also be hurt more deeply than you can imagine."

"An old puzzle? That sounds intriguing. Any idea what?"

He sighed and ran both hands through his hair. "Of course, that's the part you'd latch on to. Did you not hear the part about getting hurt? I'm not talking about normal pain here, Lawrence, but deep, soul-searing heartbreak."

Did I have enough of a heart to break anymore? I'd sacrificed everything on the altar of science. "Pain is part of life."

"So is trying to help your friends not feel it if they don't have to. Please, Lawrence, be careful."

"Thanks for the warning." I hated this sort of conversation with him. I suspected he drank before he delivered bad news so he wouldn't have to deal with his own feelings about it and so he could be deliberately vague.

"I wish I had better news. But yes, I'll see what I can do with Ashlee and Rae. Perhaps if I tell them what I saw, they'll be more amenable to helping you."

The thought of the vampires knowing anything about my future replaced the leaden cold of dread with white hot fear. I considered them as trustworthy as the average Fae, which was to say, not at all. "Please don't. Just say it has to do with the soul-eater."

"All right. I'll text you and let you know."

I studied him for a moment. "You're not telling me something."

"Can't get anything by you, can I?" He studied his hands. "There is a big darkness in your future. Typically, with people, I can see a path that fades to a sort of horizon. Yours stops abruptly and goes dark."

The warm spring breeze mocked the chill that had spread through my core. "Am I going to die?"

"No, no, that's not what that looks like. It's more like I'm being blocked from seeing more. And that scares me. It means you'll have a big choice to make, and your entire future rests on it."

"That's not comforting or specific enough for me to prepare for it. I hate it when you go horoscope-vague on me."

"Sorry, man. That's all I've got."

"Thanks, I guess." I stood. "Well, I'm going to get back." The ache to allow myself to change and fly back to Reine had turned into an urgent burning. "Please let me know when you hear from someone at the club."

"Will do. Probably won't be 'til after dark."

He walked me to the front door. Then he did something unexpected—he hugged me. "Take care of yourself, man."

"I'll try."

His warnings echoed in my head, and it battled my instincts over what I should do with Reine. As I drove off, I wondered if he'd neglected to tell me something else he'd seen or felt. Or maybe he had with the hug.

Was this the last time he expected to see me?

WHEN I ARRIVED at the hotel, I went straight up to our joined rooms. Reine looked up from her laptop on the desk when I walked in, and the tightness around her eyes and lips dimmed her smile. How much had the soul-eater taken from her in its attacks that morning? And what did it want in the end? More than just to weaken her. We still had so many questions without answers.

"Any news?" she asked. "Is Ted going to help us?"

"Yes, he'll let me know when he hears back from Ashlee or Rae."

"Good. I guess we wait, then." She glanced out the window, and her expression turned wistful.

"You don't do waiting well?" I asked.

She laughed, and the sound reminded me of water running over pebbles in a stream—young and happy, but with a cold edge. "I do waiting too well. That's part of my problem."

"What do you mean?" I sat on the bed just out of reach so I

wouldn't try to touch her. Ted's warnings flipped through my head like slides in a competitive presentation.

"I waited for several hundred years to get one chance..." She shook her head. "Never mind. It's not important."

Like hell it wasn't. "For one chance to do what?"

"Nothing."

"Do you need to go outside?" As soon as the words left my mouth, I regretted them. Even Sir Raleigh, who'd been snoozing on the bed in a perfect circle of comfortable cat-ness opened his eyes and gave me a *you idiot* glare before yawning and showing me his sharp teeth. Nice and healthy, I noticed. I knew he wasn't really a cat, but I couldn't help checking. He shifted his position and returned to sleep.

"Thanks, but I'm not a dog, Doctor Gordon." She turned back to the window. "It attacked me the first time out there." She sighed, her shoulders slumped. "I can't stay in here indefinitely. I mean, I guess I could, but it's not reasonable to expect me to."

The desire to change overtook me, and I closed my eyes and clenched my fists so I wouldn't. I could still feel my strength hadn't returned from having been poisoned and then attacked by the soul-eater, and I feared I wouldn't be able to resist the temptation to stay in gargoyle form.

"What's going on?" Reine asked. Her hand felt cool on my cheek, and in this liminal space between human and change-start, I sensed her magic flowing through me, trying to figure out what was happening. I batted her hand away.

"Don't touch me," I growled in my gargoyle voice. "You've activated my protective instincts. My inner gargoyle wants to come out and keep you safe. It's how things were before our races became enemies."

"Yes, you'd mentioned that." She drew back and returned to her chair. "He's very close to the surface today."

"Yes." Good, the voice that came out sounded more my own.

I managed to quell the change, which felt like swallowing a large pill that had gotten stuck in my esophagus, but if the sensation covered my entire body.

"What's going on with that?" she asked. "I mean, is there something else?"

I opened my eyes to see her looking at me. I wanted to believe she watched me out of caring for me, but I wasn't sure. Guilt also hit me—when she'd first arrived, I'd studied her like I feared she currently examined me.

"I'm not sure." I rubbed my eyes, which itched. I really wanted to thump my chest, where my heart thudded in a sludge of anxiety, confusion, and something else I couldn't name out of fear it wouldn't be reciprocated.

My phone dinged with a text, and I pulled it out. Ted —*"You're in. Get to the club at dusk. She'll see you when she's ready."*

"Oh, good."

"What?"

I tried and failed to hide my grin at the thought of her in a skin-tight dress like she'd worn a couple of nights previously. "We're going clubbing tonight."

7

REINE

After Ted's text, Lawrence went into his room to rest and do some work for the CPDC. He didn't know what projects might be suspended, but he didn't want to take the chance his funding would be cut. I didn't bother to try to figure out the intricacies and politics of it all. None if it had anything to do with me or my Fae business.

The girls sent me text updates, and it sounded like the soul-eater had gone quiet again. I knew it wouldn't sleep. It would be stalking, watching, planning... I wished I knew what it wanted with me, but that kind of creature didn't answer direct questions. As in, they never answered them. Dark Fae creatures took plotting and amorality to extreme lengths. If it wanted me to know its end game, it would have told me.

The vampire club owner would see us when she was ready. Because vampires didn't take appointments? It could end up being a long night, so I decided to lie on the bed and let my body rest even if my mind wouldn't. I texted Kestrel and Sparkle to call me if something major happened. Otherwise, I hoped they would enjoy themselves. Kestrel needed a break.

I got comfortable on my back, and Sir Raleigh crawled on to

my chest, where he curled up and purred. I stroked his soft fur, and the sound and sensations soon lulled me to sleep, my left hand across his back.

After a period of black sleep, a stage where I could tell I was asleep but had no memory of being so, I emerged into a dream. Mist surrounded me, but instead of as previously, when I struggled up a rocky hill I couldn't see, I floated between faded green grass and a sky so dim it made the Faerie sun into a moon.

Somehow, I'd come home again, if only in a dream. The mist faded, and I recognized where I was—in the Gray Space, or area between the territories of the light and dark Fae. Here different kinds of chaos magic mingled to form the Mist of Deception.

I knew I had to be extra careful. How had I gotten here? This was the territory of the gray Fae, whom neither the light nor dark wanted to acknowledge the existence of, but whom we all secretly feared.

Sir Raleigh appeared beside me in his grimalkin form, a large black panther with one white paw and leathery wings that had looked like a bat's when I'd seen them on Earth, but now resembled dragon wings. He glanced up at me with green eyes and made a chirp as he would in cat form. It sounded ridiculous coming from such an intimidating creature, and I sensed he wanted to put me at ease, let me know he would protect me, or at least try. That didn't help me feel more comfortable, and again the questions of who had sent him to me—and what they'd want in return—came to mind.

Well, we were here now, so I might as well see what he had to show me.

My feet touched the grass, and I followed him, careful not to step from the path he led me along. If someone were to have watched us, they would have seen us take a meandering path through the tall grass. A straight line would have led me into traps the gray laid to keep trespassers out of their territory.

Curious, I knelt and tried to pluck a blade from its stem, but it didn't release. Instead, it left a thin red line on my thumb that I healed before anything could smell my blood.

Razor grass—it appeared benign, but it would lacerate legs before you even felt it. I pressed my palm to a blank spot of earth beside it and found that also to be deceiving, as my hand passed through it. So that was the infamous dimensional quicksand that could suck you in and send you somewhere you might not be able to come back from.

Sir Raleigh turned his head to me, and I read the question in the twitch of his ears, *"Satisfied now?"* He cocked his head to indicate we should keep moving, and although I wanted to explore what I could from my supposedly safe spot on the path, no one knew what sort of Gray creatures would be called forth by the very presence of a light Fae. Sir Raleigh in his Grimalkin form was frightening enough, and there was the soul-eater. I didn't think I wanted to meet their cousins.

We moved toward a forest where the low-hanging branches obscured the view of what lay inside with hungry, green shadows. A branch snapped within, and I jumped. Sir Raleigh's fur stood up in spines along his back, and he turned left before we passed under the first tree.

As we skirted the forest, the sound of voices came to me. At first, they sounded like they were far off, and I couldn't make out anything. The mist muffled sounds and obfuscated the direction they came from. As Sir Raleigh led me closer to the speakers, I could make out a man and a woman speaking, and then my chest clenched when I could hear clearly enough to recognize them.

"Time is running out, Ellerin," my grandmother said. "In every sense. I cannot stay in the Gray Space much longer."

The deep well of sorrow and longing that I kept covered opened up within my soul, and I placed my hands to my cheeks and found tears. It had been so long since I'd seen her in person. I'd dreamed of her—had it been a dream? —and she'd warned me of a plot against her, but that had been a vision. This felt real.

I wanted to rush to her, but Sir Raleigh blocked me. *"Wait,"* his eyes said. He pushed his head under my hand, and I calmed as I stroked it.

"I am aware of that, Tatiana, but my hands are tied, and no one can know about our meeting. The dark Fae court isn't talking about anything related to our issue, and it's not like I can ask directly." It took me a moment to figure out the speaker from his voice—the man who appeared to be following me, but who wouldn't give me his name. At least now I knew it— Ellerin. It wasn't like my grandmother to be so careless as to reveal another Fae's name. Or perhaps she'd been asserting her power over him.

"We still don't know who has sicced the creature on my granddaughter, and I don't like her being in danger. She's the only reason I summoned you to meet with me."

If she cared for me so much, why hadn't she allowed me back into Faerie?

Ellerin snorted. Since he was Fae, he somehow made it sound charming. "I've been keeping an eye on her, don't worry. She is doing well. She has gathered her allies around her, and she is working on the problem from her own angles."

"And will she share what she knows with you? She can't suspect your relationship to her."

Relationship? I'd never seen him in my life before he'd talked to me in the Stirling Airport.

No, that wasn't right. There was something tickling at the back of my brain. I let it be. After five hundred years, I'd learned that memories would emerge from the morass in their own time.

Wait, he'd addressed her by her first name, not with any

honorific. Not just anyone could do that and live to tell about it. Who was this Ellerin?

"She does not know who I am, don't worry."

"Good." That one syllable had the weight of her entire authority behind it, the verbal equivalent of a metal door slamming shut. Whoever he was to me, they wouldn't discuss it any more.

Leaves rustled in a spot about ten feet away, at least from what I could tell. The mist was returning, obscuring distance again, and every hair on my body stood on end when Sir Raleigh turned and sniffed the air, his mouth partially open in the feline flehmen position. He smelled something interesting.

Then a snort or snuffle of some kind, this time just out of view. Right, time to go. Sir Raleigh agreed and bumped against me, driving me away from the clandestine meeting. I had been lucky they hadn't sensed me.

Before their voices disappeared behind me, I thought I heard her ask him, "Has the grimalkin...?"

I stopped, but Sir Raleigh kept me moving. He mustn't have wanted me to hear that part.

The hum of the hotel climate control system pulled me from the dream/vision/visitation, and I woke with my hand atop a purring Sir Raleigh. The shadows outside had lengthened and the light turned the orange-gold of early evening.

I rolled over to see Lawrence sitting on the bed beside me.

"Are you all right?" he asked. "I've been trying to wake you for half an hour, but the cat wouldn't let me touch you."

"I'm fine. What do you need?"

"Have you forgotten? We're meeting with Ashlee Wyatt tonight. Time to get ready."

I rolled to a sitting position and took a moment to allow my head to stop spinning. Once it cleared, light raced through my body and made my limbs tingle. My brief sojourn in Faerie had returned some of my strength. I reached for Sir Raleigh, who sat and bathed his white paw. He gave me an innocent look, but I knew better. He'd acted the ally, but he'd also kept me from hearing information about him. Had my grandmother sent him? Or had the mysterious Fae—I had to grasp at the wisps of memory that tried to fade like a dream to remember his name, Ellerin—been responsible for Sir Raleigh's appearance? He'd certainly been interested in making sure I kept the grimalkin nearby to protect me. Or was that to spy on me?

So many questions. I went into the bathroom and splashed cold water on my face to finish waking myself up. I could ponder them later. I'd need all my wits about me to handle Ashlee Wyatt.

I DECIDED that midnight blue would be a more appropriate color for the vampire club, somber but still with silver sparkling thread woven throughout the long dress in intricate patterns. The gown hugged my curves, hung off one shoulder, and had a long slit up the left leg. With my hair piled atop my head and sapphires in my ears and at my throat, I felt ready to slay anything, even a soul-eater.

Lawrence wore his black slacks with a matching jacket that had been tailored to show off his broad shoulders and trim waist. Underneath it, he wore a dark gray shirt and no tie.

"Gargoyle colors?" I teased.

He didn't grin back. "Are you ready?"

"Yes." I pouted, although I didn't like pouting. But there had been a flare of interest in his eyes when he'd first seen me, so I knew I still attracted him. What had gotten into him? Or was he still trying not to garg out? Damn, I'd hoped my ensemble portrayed feminine strength and power. Or maybe it enhanced his protectiveness. I resisted the urge to twitch my shoulders at the thought. While it would be nice to have someone who had my back, the idea of protection felt smothering. I was a Fae, for Hades' sake. And not just any Fae, a royal Fae who somehow managed to be caught up in a Faerie plot even though I hadn't physically been in Faerie for over three hundred years.

Sometimes it was hard to be a Fae.

Rhys walked in and raised his gaze from his phone. "Looking sharp, sis. Where are you going?"

"To meet with a vampire."

"Ugh." Rhys wrinkled his nose. "I thought those were stuck in the Collective Unconscious and Nightmare Realm. What's one doing here?"

"Running a night club," Lawrence said. "Now if you'll excuse us."

Rhys mock-saluted and preceded us out of the room. "Just thought I'd make a quick report. All has been quiet downstairs, although there were a couple of suspicious incidents. People asking out-of-character questions at panels, and one getting asked to leave for being drunk, although once they got outside, he swore up and down he hadn't been drinking."

We'd walked into the hallway, and Sir Raleigh, who rode on my shoulder for now, didn't react to anything, so I suspected the soul-eater wasn't around up there.

"What is it doing?" Lawrence asked.

I mashed the elevator button with extra force. "Learning. It's learning about humans and how they see Fae so it can use the knowledge against me." But why would it care about human knowledge? Was that part of its strategy to trap me, or was it acting on its own?

That was the frightening thing about dark Fae creatures— they often adopted their own agenda beyond that of the Fae who had summoned them. That's just what we needed, a rogue soul-eater.

We made it downstairs and through the lobby without any incident. I thought I could feel it watching me, but Sir Raleigh, although alert, didn't show any sign he sensed it, so I suspected it waited. But for what?

Kestrel and Sparkle caught up to us while the valets fetched Lawrence's car. Kestrel didn't do anything to recall our interaction from earlier, so I decided to stay quiet about it as well.

"Wow." Sparkle looked us up and down. "Y'all look great. Where are you going?"

"To talk to a potential ally," I said. "Any news?"

"No," Kestrel said. "It's all quiet." Her phone buzzed, and she sighed when she read the message on the screen. "Great, that's my dad. He wants me home for dinner." When she raised her head, I saw her eyes had gone shiny with tears, and when she spoke, she sounded very young. "I... This sounds horrible, but I don't want to go home."

Sparkle put an arm around her and hugged her. "I know it's hard. But your dad needs you."

Kestrel nodded. "I know, I know. But I don't think I can be in that house. It just doesn't feel right."

"No, and it won't for a while," Lawrence said. This time when his eyes darkened, it was with remembered pain that floated through the space between us. "But you can handle it. We'll drop you on our way downtown."

"Is it the convertible?" she asked.

Lawrence cracked a small smile. "Yes, it's the convertible."

"All right. I guess that will do."

A valet pulled Lawrence's black convertible up, and we let Kestrel get in the back, then I took the passenger seat. Lawrence got in and let the top down.

The balmy spring breeze teased my hair, but I didn't mind. It would be windblown by the time we got where we were going, and I hoped it would end up more on the "adorably tousled" side of the scale.

None of us said anything—it was hard to around the wind —and we dropped Kestrel off at her parents' house without incident. John came out and waved, then mimed to Lawrence he was going to text something to him. Lawrence waved back and gave him a thumbs-up.

"Did he get the toxicology results back?" I asked when we pulled away. Residential speed allowed us to have a conversation.

He shook his head, and his phone dinged.

I waited until he was stopped at the light that would let us out of the neighborhood and on to a four-lane road, then asked, "Aren't you going to look? Maybe that's the tox results."

"I will once we get there. We have a no cell phone use while driving law here."

Right, he was a rule-follower. I acknowledged the irra-tionality of the impatience I felt—it wasn't like he could do anything about the contents of the text, but he could take a peek, see if John had found out something about the toxicology test.

I sighed and focused on the trees around us and the energy of the red clay soil and thousand growing things. I appreciated the green-ness of Atlanta and its suburbs, and the trees whis-pered their greetings to me.

Lawrence clenched his jaw, and so I asked, "What?"

"You know what. That sound..." He shook his head. "What are they telling you?"

"Hello, mostly. They're being *polite*."

"It would be more polite for them to stay quiet and not give me nightmares," he grumbled.

"Seriously!" I exploded. "What has gotten into you? Did something happen while I was asleep?"

"Other than a deadly creature stalking a convention, one of my friends being killed by one of my other friends and none of us really knowing why, and you volunteering to babysit Kestrel, then leaving her on her own?"

I sat back and crossed my arms against the chill between us.

"I told you I needed to rest, and Kestrel was fine. She needed something to do since she obviously wasn't handling things well on her own." I sulked for a minute, then recalled what Rhys had said—he thought I was acting more human than Fae. He hadn't used the words, but I could guess how the conversation would go if I were to tell him what had happened. He'd say that whenever Fae tried to act too human, it backfired. But between leaving Kestrel to manage on her own and pushing Lawrence to break the law, I'd been acting more Fae than human, and that hadn't gone well, either.

Then the little voice in my brain, the one that had emerged after a hundred years living in this realm, piped up. *You could be more sympathetic. Remember what you told Rhys—Lawrence has been through a lot.*

Right, but I need him to talk to me if that's the case, not hold it all in, then blow up about the trees saying hi.

Uh, you got impatient and blew up at him first.

I hated it when the little voice was right, but I didn't feel ready to apologize. Maybe a rift between us would be for the best. I was planning to return to Faerie and leave him, after all.

Unfortunately, those plans didn't feel quite as comfortable as they previously had, either. That scared me more than anything, so I wrapped my ice queen Fae persona around myself and didn't say anything until we arrived at the club. As he had before, Sir Raleigh disappeared into my purse, and I allowed the bouncer to open the convertible door. I made sure to allow my leg to peek out through the slit in my dress as I exited the car.

Rae met us at the door. Once again, his eyes were hidden behind mirrored sunglasses with white frames, and this evening his hair had been dyed light purple to match his suit.

"Did the monster come with you?" Rae asked without saying hello.

I resisted the urge to ask which one, considering Sir Raleigh could count as a monster, but I knew he meant the soul-eater. "No, not as far as I know."

"Good. Mistress Ashlee isn't ready for you yet, but she's instructed the bartender to give you your favorites, and there's a table for you."

He gestured for us to follow him. Although it wasn't yet eight o'clock, the club had already half-filled. We got several glares when the bartender served us right away, and then when we walked to the table we'd sat at two nights and what felt like a lifetime ago. Unfortunately, we had one of the same problems as previously—the soul-eater—although we'd managed to solve the other one, the mystery of who had leaked the CLS vector and why. Not that that had gone like anyone expected.

Lawrence seemed to relax as he sipped his drink.

"What is that, again?" I asked.

"An Old-Fashioned," he said. "A classic." He shook his head and put it on the table. "Like me, someone said."

I wanted to ask what he meant, what the text said, what he was thinking... The *thump-thump-thump* of the music surrounded us in a cocoon of sound and gave us some semblance of privacy.

I studied his face, which the lights of the club illuminated in flashes of color and mood. Red—annoyed. Blue—sad. Purple—perplexed. Yellow—pensive. White—naked. Wait, what had that last one been? Not naked as in unclothed, but naked as in vulnerable, open, honest...

I shivered at the unfamiliarity of the emotions. I knew anger and dislike—my mother had seen to that, and I'd learned I'd rather not know how people and Fae really felt toward me. About other things, sure. I'd found it safer to assume everyone would betray me eventually, which helped me not feel, well, naked.

Something warm touched my hand, and I found Lawrence's

fingers clasping mine. "You're cold," he said. "Should've brought a sweater."

I smiled and resisted the urge to tease him about being protective again.

"Would you like to dance?" he asked and waved toward the dance floor, where a few couples gyrated, lost in the music. Their desire showed on their faces, the way their gazes and hands flicked off and around each other in their own dances.

Could I do that? Could we?

Why not? It might be the only way we could safely explore our feelings.

"Yes."

8

LAWRENCE

"We're going to dance," I told Rae, who had somehow materialized at our table to ask if we wanted more to drink.

"Very good. The lady may leave her purse here. No one will touch it."

I knew that to be the case. If they did, they'd have their hand bitten off by an angry grimalkin, but I didn't mention that. "Thank you."

She didn't let go of my hand as we rose and made our way through the growing crowd to the dance floor. Thankfully, only a few other couples occupied it.

We faced each other, now holding both hands.

"Do you know how to dance?" she asked.

"No. I don't know what I was thinking." Only that I had to stop her from studying me so intently. Her scrutiny reminded me too much of what Ted had told me that afternoon, and it felt as though she had been prying my secrets out of my head and pulling them apart. Or maybe I wished she would so I didn't have to bear the burden of Ted's predictions alone. "Do you?"

"I do, but it's been a while. None of that." She inclined her head toward a couple making complex movements with their arms and legs. "Hold on."

She walked over to the deejay and spoke in his ear. She held her hand to the side of her mouth so he could hear her, but the gesture also kept me from being able to read her lips to see what she said. As she walked back to me, her long left leg playing a tantalizing peekaboo through the slit in her dress, the music slowed, then changed to something multilayered in a minor key. She took my hands again.

"Follow my lead, Gargoyle. Try not to have stone feet."

"Challenge accepted, Milady."

She placed my left hand on her waist, and I steadied her as she leaned back, her left leg rubbing mine as she stretched it behind me. She flung her head back, giving me a tempting glimpse of her white throat, then snapped back to upright in a motion too fast to be human. I barely had time for the thought that that movement resembled something Rhys would do with his Fae defiantly on show. Then her magic picked up my feet to match hers in a complex pattern of movements.

Her magic or mine? No time to think, just hold on and notice and feel.

The room whirled by in a mix of colored light and sound. The bass had returned, punctuating our movements. Clasp, turn, brush, dip, swirl... My mind couldn't keep up with the verbs, as much as it wanted to analyze and remember. Through it all, her green eyes blazed when our faces drew closer together. Her eyelids dipped demurely when we moved apart, and then she'd slay me with a side glance, and I'd have to swallow, remind myself to breathe and keep up.

A bead of sweat ran down my right temple, but I had no time to brush it aside as my hands were needed elsewhere. All over her body, or close to it, as she engaged in another complex dip movement, and I might have held tightly as much to steady myself as her. My inner gargoyle growled in pleasure, and I had to clench my jaw so I wouldn't join him. Amusement flashed over her face, and her pink lips curled into an unfiltered expression of joy that I had to answer.

"Are you actually having fun, Doctor Gordon?" she whispered as we glided across the floor, long legs and torsos pressed.

"Yes, actually. If this is fun, I need to do it more often."

She laughed as she spun away, and then when she came back into my arms, her back to my front, the music stopped, and she tilted her head back.

I gave into the urge and lightly pressed my lips to hers. As before, the sense of something locking into place elongated the moment with a sense of homecoming. Applause erupted around us and within me, and I turned her so she pressed fully into me without losing contact.

Rae's words served as the bucket of cold water that separated us. "Miss Wyatt will see you now."

RAE LEFT us in the upper room we'd been in before with a fresh set of drinks, an Old-Fashioned for me and white wine for Reine. She'd started with red, then switched to white.

"I need something without tannins after all that." She'd fanned her face with one hand, and she still smiled. I hadn't seen her so relaxed, well, ever.

"You're both very good dancers," Rae had grudgingly admitted. "Thank you for the show."

I shrugged. "The credit goes to her. I was just following."

The air in the upstairs space cooled my skin, and I ran a finger under my collar to allow my neck some relief. While I could work up a good sweat during my workouts, this felt different.

"Are you all right?" Reine asked. She dabbed at her face with a tissue she'd fished from her reticule.

"I think so. Just warm."

"Me, too. That was impressive. You were able to keep up with everything I threw at you." She lifted her glass in a toast.

"Likewise."

We'd been standing a few feet apart, and I took the two steps to close the distance between us and clink my glass against hers. How had she interpreted the kiss? Did she think it had been a product of the moment, or had she recognized it as more? Had I overstepped the bounds of appropriateness?

She turned away, her cheeks pink. The question of what she was thinking stuck at the back of my tongue. I had to sort those questions out for myself before I could talk to her about it, but it was damn hard not to kiss her again when she tilted her head toward me. The Fae calculation had returned to her eyes, but she lifted her hand. I readied myself to lean into it when she caressed my cheek, but instead she held the back of her hand to my forehead.

"You feel a little warm. Are you having any fever symptoms? I'm sorry—I should have taken into account that you've had a rough week."

And with her return to doctor mode, the magic bubble around us popped, and I stepped back. "I told you, I'm fine. That was an aerobic workout." Now my inner gargoyle growled again, this time in resentment that we hadn't continued the aerobic workout in a bedroom. Or on one of the plush divans or chairs in the space. Plus, it wasn't her job to protect me, but the other way around—even if, according to Ted, I'd need protecting soon.

I resented the complication of the situation. It wasn't supposed to be like this, but Fae-Gargoyle relations had been fraught with pitfalls and traps for centuries. I needed to remember that, especially since she could seal my doom.

"All right." The coolness had returned to her tone, and a sinking sensation in the pit of my stomach gave me the answer as to whether I'd done something stupid kissing her without her consent...or did it? Fae could be so hard to read and held grudges. She had become angry with me for not looking at John's text while driving. Another difference between us and our species—gargoyles followed rules, Fae bent them. She could take command on the dance floor because she had superior knowledge there, but I would control my actions otherwise, thank you very much.

I did take my phone out and read the text—*Heard from lab. Tox results still pending.*

"And...?" she asked.

"Updating me that there's no news. Definitely not worth getting a ticket over."

"I see." She turned and walked toward the windows overlooking the club. The tension in her shoulders made me want to go rub them and help her relax, but she'd practically left a corridor of cold in her wake.

All right, that comment about the ticket had been unnecessary.

I turned to see Ashlee Wyatt standing behind me. She'd arrived with typical vampire silence. "Oh, now isn't this delicious? All these complex feelings. Why don't you two just fuck and get it over with?"

9

REINE

At the vampire's words, I whirled around with Fae speed. If there was one thing I hated more than gargoyles, it was vampires who thought they had the upper hand. Anger at Lawrence flashed through me for making the situation more complicated than it needed to be.

What had he been thinking with that kiss? What had I?

We hadn't, that was the problem. Gods, I'd be dreaming about that dance for months. He'd only needed a slight magical nudge, which I had to keep gentle because his magic had alternately tried to fight with and take over mine. Of course, my mind had gone to the next logical question—what would he be like in bed? Then he'd opened his mouth, and his condescension had dampened my desire. Not eliminated completely, alas, but I didn't think he'd agree to being gagged so he wouldn't say anything stupid. Or maybe he'd surprise me and be into that. Who in Hades knew?

Now we had another problem. Ashlee Wyatt stood in front of a black velvet curtain, and I catalogued the impression she made. The black sleeveless high-necked dress with keyhole chest and long black satin gloves helped her to blend in and gave the impression of a floating head, shoulders, and cleavage. She wore her hair up in a style from the eighteenth century, which produced an interesting contrast.

"You wanted to meet with me?" she asked with red, smiling lips and fangs she didn't bother to hide from us this time. All predator, no mercy.

This would be a tough negotiation. Luckily, Fae excelled at those.

"Yes, thank you," I forced my shoulders to relax and my lips to soften into a grateful grin. "And thank you for taking such good care of us."

She inclined her head, but her reply created more questions. "It's a good thing you have friends in low places who are willing to pick up your tab."

I glanced at Lawrence. Could she mean Ted? Lawrence looked as confused as I felt, and I recalled I'd seen the gray Fae gentleman here previously. Could this be how he helped us?

"I see. Well, thank you for accommodating them."

"What can I do for you, Princess?" She allowed some impatience into her tone. "As you can see, it's a busy night here, and you've created a certain frenzy on my dance floor. Quite impressive, by the way. We don't often have paranormals perform for us."

The way she said it made it sound like we'd done some sort of pornographic dance, but now that I knew to feel for it, I sensed the heightened sexual tension in the place. Damn. Hadn't meant for that to happen. To any of us. Well, not them, anyway.

"I am here to take you up on your offer to help us capture the soul-eater," I said, starting with a general and neutral request, hoping she'd take the bait and see it as her idea.

"I see. And what will you offer in return?"

Fucking vampires. "You will be able to keep the creature in your menagerie. I will not insist upon its return to Faerie for punishment." I hated to give up the freedom of another Fae creature, but spending its existence in the vampire's menagerie would be preferable to punishment at my grandmother's guards' hands. Assuming one of them hadn't helped to summon it and unleash it in this realm.

That would be yet another reason to not allow it to return to Faerie... plots within plots within plots.

Ashlee tapped her red lips with a matching fingernail. Well, if you got it, own it, I supposed. I watched her as she pondered the conditions of my offer. Or perhaps she wanted to make me wait and squirm. That wouldn't happen. Fae had infinite patience and excelled at allowing other creatures—including fellow Fae—to spool out far enough to hang themselves with their own lies, suspicions, and doubts.

Ashlee's white-blonde hair and mine had the same coloring, although hers had a black streak at one temple and was straight, whereas mine had a slightly gold sheen and curled softly. How old was she? At least a couple hundred Earth years —no telling how old in whatever time the nightmare realm counted. Her ice-blue eyes went predator, flat, and she smiled. I braced for her counter-offer.

"While I appreciate the opportunity to have such a creature in my menagerie, I feel the balance isn't met." She walked to the window and continued speaking to us over her shoulder, an empress surveying her kingdom.

"How so?" Lawrence asked.

"Recall, this creature killed one of my men in an effort to threaten you, Princess." She turned with vampire speed and allowed anger to distort her features for the space of a blink. Yes, she could be scary if she wanted to. "And disturbed Rae. As you can probably guess, nothing disturbs Rae. He is the model of Japanese reserve."

I retreated into formal Fae speak. "Yes, and for that I am truly saddened for the loss of your man and Rae's distress."

No way would I take responsibility. I couldn't control the creature.

"Thus, I have my own beef with the creature, as the humans like to say, and I could capture it in my own time, wait for it to hunt here again. The question is, what will you give me for helping you on your timeline? I sense some urgency in your request."

Lawrence and I looked at each other. We hadn't discussed how much to reveal to the vampire, and I sorted through the possibilities.

"Remember," she continued, "I gave you a valuable piece of information the last time we met—how to get in touch with Robert Cannon."

Ugh, right, she had done that for us. The balance was definitely in her favor, so I decided upon a risky move—honesty.

"The creature is currently stalking Fae-Con," I said. "Until we can contain it, all the humans there are in danger."

"Call off the 'Con."

I wished Lawrence would place his hand on my back so I could calm myself easily, but he didn't. Right, we were in a classic Fae-gargoyle disagreement.

He did answer, though. "We've tried, but the humans aren't cooperating."

"Ah, yes, they often don't, do they?" She sighed. "Well, then, I will help you catch this creature."

"And in return...?" I asked.

"You will allow me to drink from you, Princess."

Her words shouldn't have surprised me, but they made me rock back on my high heels, and, "Never!" flew from my lips.

"Why not?" She crossed her arms. "Do you not think me worthy?"

"Because, because, Fae don't *do* that," I sputtered and swallowed around the knot of revulsion that had risen from my gut to my throat. "We don't allow anyone to take anything from us."

"Which is why this would even out our debt." She spoke calmly, and I cursed internally at my fluttering heartbeat and sense of panic at the thought of allowing a vampire to sample my blood.

"We have reasons, Miss Wyatt," I said. "Good reasons."

"Such as...?"

"It would taint us, and we wouldn't be allowed back into Faerie." All right, I didn't know that with certainty, but that's one thing I'd been told.

"Not true. I have heard tales of vampires drinking from your kind and healing them so no one would know."

There went my argument about marks and scars. Some humans wore theirs proudly during times in history when vampires had been allowed to roam freely outside the Collective Unconscious. A Fae would never show they'd been bitten. Nor would they allow any other Fae to know.

I thought of another argument. "I don't know what it would do to you. You may become addicted to Fae blood."

She laughed. "What do you take me for, Princess? Vampires are only addicted to beauty, wealth, and blood in a general sense. You have all three, but I don't see myself needing more than the one drink."

Lawrence moved to my side. Ah, there was his hand on my back. I took a deep breath.

When he spoke, his tone had a resonance that revealed his protective instincts had kicked in. I envied how reasonable he sounded. "Why are you so insistent upon her blood? You can drink from me in return for helping us."

"Tempting, Gargoyle," she said. "Very tempting, but not the same. Think it over, Princess. You'll soon see that this is your only viable course of action."

"What do you mean?"

She folded her hands in front of her. On another woman, the gesture would have appeared demure. On her, calculating.

"The only creatures who have a chance to defeat a soul-eater who preys on the life energy of those around it are the ones who are already dead." Now she spread her hands, a model of reasonableness. "Unless you know of any other undead beings, your only choice is to accept my bargain."

Hades, I hated it when someone out-Fae-bargained a Fae.

"Very well." I ground the words out. "I will consider it."

"Don't wait too long, Princess." Now she portrayed earnestness, but her sly smile gave her away. "It grows stronger, and you weaker. Don't delay until your blood is no longer sufficient payment."

LAWRENCE and I left the club, me in a daze, him radiating fury.

Once we retrieved his car, I allowed Sir Raleigh to emerge from my purse and curl up on my lap. He purred as I stroked his soft fur and tried to calm the whirling of my thoughts.

Lawrence stayed silent until we turned on to Peachtree, a strangely named street considering there were no peach trees, and asked, "You're considering it, aren't you?"

I buried my face in my hands. "I don't know what else to do." Ellerin's words echoed in my brain—*"We're running out of time. So is she."* Is this what he meant? That soon I would no longer be able to defeat the soul-eater because it grew so strong?

"I wasn't all right with the risk to you before, but now it seems the safer choice would be to try to talk to it, see what it wants."

Sir Raleigh nudged my elbow, and I returned to petting him. "It's a Fae creature, Lawrence. It's not going to be direct with me." Plus, I didn't want to have any contact with it, even through the supposedly safe portal of a séance with a strong medium.

"No, but if anyone could decode what it's trying not to tell you, it's another Fae."

I turned my head to see his expression since his words, spoken with patience, also conveyed frustration and...reluctance?

"You don't like the idea of allying with the vampires or of me talking to the soul-eater."

"No, I told you, it's risky. Both are."

"No," I mimicked. "You're not happy with me acting as a Fae."

"You have to admit I have a good reason."

"Which is...?"

A sigh. "We can talk when we get back to the hotel."

We slid under the bright LED street lights, and I pondered my choices. By the time we arrived back at the hotel, I still hadn't come up with an answer. There was no way I'd allow Ashlee Wyatt to drink from me. She hadn't told me her reasons for wanting to, for one. I should have asked, but I'd been too shocked by the request.

But every contact with the soul-eater had left me weakened, and it had proven itself clever. What if it had a way to get to me through a séance?

I intended to move quickly through the lobby and to our rooms, but Lady Sparkle jumped up from one of the chairs across from the lobby doors when we walked in.

"There you are! I need to talk to you." When she reached us, she added, "Actually, Samir wants to talk to you."

I groaned. "Let me guess...Rhys."

She nodded. We followed her to the registration area, which at this time of night only held two volunteers prepping for the next day and an irritated-looking Samir.

"What can I do for you?" I examined him as best I could for signs of possession and didn't see any. Plus, if the soul-eater had been lurking around, Sir Raleigh would have growled from my purse. Or would he? I opened it, presumably to fish out my phone, and found the cat had vanished. Damn. "Please make it quick. I need to get back to my room."

"This will only take a second. I've had complaints about your brother."

I groaned. "What sorts of complaints?"

"That's the thing. Nothing specific. Only that he's creeping some people out."

"This is ridiculous," Lawrence snapped. "Cons are supposed to be inclusive of people who are different. If he hasn't done anything, then what's the problem?"

"This is going to sound vague," Samir said with a sigh and rubbed his eyes. "A couple of women did say he'd been following them too closely, but they couldn't explain what they meant."

"Probably that he moved like a Fae, not a human," I muttered, then, at a volume he could hear me, "Fine, I'll talk to him."

"Thanks. By the way, have you had any luck with your other problem?"

"No." I turned and walked away before I could add, "No thanks to you."

Lawrence followed me. "What are you going to do now?"

I texted Rhys to let him know I was coming to see him and to meet me at his room.

"Already here. Have company."

I sighed. Of course he did. "Talk to my brother. Then I'll join you in our room. We need to discuss some things." Like that kiss on the dance floor. I'd been able to dismiss the first one since it had been flirty and playful, but could be attributed to an experiment, nothing serious. This second one... I'd felt his internal gargoyle stretching its wings to cover me with them. I didn't know if I liked it or disliked it. Yet more things to sort through.

Lawrence said goodbye to me when I got off on Rhys' floor, and the flare of desire in his eyes made me wonder whether he'd thought about kissing me again. I certainly had. That was the problem with kisses—they could be addictive.

I knocked on Rhys' room door, and when he opened it, he was pulling a shirt on. A blushing young African American woman wearing steampunk gear and carrying fairy wings ducked under his arm, and I stepped back to let her through.

"Thanks for the wonderful evening, Love," she said in a Caribbean accent.

"Any time," Rhys purred. I resisted the urge to roll my eyes.

"See you tomorrow?"

"Definitely."

"Bye, then."

"Bye." They engaged in a long goodbye snog, and this time I did roll my eyes.

She flitted down the hall, and Rhys held the door open for me. "You had something to talk to me about, Sis?"

I took in his hotel room. Somehow, he'd managed to stock up a full bar complete with glasses, some that still had brown and clear liquids in them.

"What in Hades have you been doing?"

He grinned. "Looking for the soul-eater among the 'Con-goers, of course."

"Where, in their pants? Please tell me that whatever's been going on in here is consensual. No glamours or other tricks."

"Absolutely not." He put his right hand to his chest and widened his eyes, a picture of innocence. "These American girls dig a guy with a scar and an accent."

Trust my brother to figure out how to get in girls' pants, skirts, corsets—whatever—in record time. He'd already gotten more action in an evening than I had in a hundred years, and fury born of sexual frustration exploded in my chest. "And have you found out anything useful under their clothes or at the backs of their throats?"

"Not yet, but I'm happy to keep searching."

Gods, I wanted to slap the smirk off his face, but I settled with clenching my fists instead. "You have to tone it down. There have been complaints. This isn't fifty years ago, when people looked the other way when men were stupidly aggressive. And thank Goddess for that."

He held up his hands. "I haven't done anything wrong. I may have thought I saw signs of possession in a couple of girls and went in for a closer peek, but no worries. Nothing there."

I rubbed my temples. "Let me guess, except for some exceptional corset-lifted cleavage or low-cut fairy dresses?"

"Well, we think the soul-eater is a he, right? Wouldn't blame the bloke. Some of the costumes are..." He kissed his fingertips, then spread them. "Magnificent."

I shoved him hard, and he fell backward on to the bed. "You're not listening to me, Rhys. You need to back off. You're going to get us all kicked out if you continue." I allowed lightning to spark at my fingertips and pointed at his lower abdomen. "Do I need to do more to get your attention?"

He held up his hands again. "All right, all right. I thought I was helping."

I so badly wanted to say, "No, you didn't," but I again bit my tongue and closed my fist over the sparks. "It's not that hard." I counted off my instructions on my fingers. "First, lay off the girls. If they come to you, fine. But for Fae's sake, stop following them."

"Fine," he spat, although his expression crept into sulky territory.

"Second," I continued, "you have to be more aware of how you move. People notice if you walk like a Fae, not a human, and it creeps them out."

"Fine. I'll slow down, move like an inferior being."

I doubted it would make him suffer as much as his rolled eyes and beleaguered tone intimated.

"Third, actually *try* to help, not this half-assed effort you're making. It's not enough. That thing is out there, and it's dangerous, and it's after me."

"Right, right, I hear you. I'll help. Is that all?" He glanced at the clock. "I have another, ah, appointment in a few, and I need to grab a shower."

"Yes. Don't do anything stupid."

"When have I ever—don't answer that."

I pointedly looked at his scar.

"You're channeling Mum again," he grumbled.

I had nothing to say to that, so I turned and let myself out. As I stalked down the hall, I fumed, but I didn't know who I was angrier at—him for being his usual dumb self or myself for losing control and shoving him. What had my mother been thinking, sending him here? Had she forgotten how useless he was?

No, he'd always been her favorite, for some weird reason. She probably thought he'd come in and save the day, and then my grandmother would have to let him into Faerie, scar and all.

I pushed the elevator button, and my shoulder blades snapped straight as a cold, invisible finger traced its way across my exposed upper back.

10

___

REINE

"You're so beautiful," the voice hissed into my ear. "I cannot wait to possess you."

With a yowl, Sir Raleigh appeared at my feet and arched up into Halloween cat mode. I summoned my shield magic, flinging the soul-eater back. I didn't know how long I could keep it up, so I grabbed the cat and ran toward the stairs. No way would I be stuck in an elevator with that thing.

The metal fire door slammed behind me as I entered the stairwell. My heels pinched my feet, so I kicked them off and ran up the first flight of stairs but then had to stop. I gasped for air, struggling to fill my lungs, like in a sleep paralysis-tinged nightmare. The door opened and closed without anyone visible coming in, and Sir Raleigh hissed and squirmed, which made me drop him. He looked up at me like, *"Go, stupid,"* so I went, but I had to stop and rest at the landing that led to the door out to the next floor.

The words came into my mind. *"Your little pet isn't enough to protect you, Princess."*

With a pained yowl, Sir Raleigh bounded up the stairs behind me. Then—brave creature—he arched again and grew into the dragon-winged panther I'd seen in Faerie and once before.

One more floor, two more flights of stairs. Could I do it?

Black footprints appeared on the first, then second steps on the flight behind me. I had to try.

Sir Raleigh swiped at something, and a hiss of pain bounced off the concrete and metal.

"You'll pay for that."

My grimalkin yowled again, and the sound drove me forward. I checked behind me to see him pacing back and forth and snapping and swiping at something. Claw marks appeared on his coat, then disappeared. How much damage could gray Fae creatures do to each other?

"Come on!"

Ellerin, dressed in his usual gray suit, stood on the next landing. He wore a fedora like a gangster from some old movie. He held out a hand, and I took it.

He hauled me up to the intermediate landing. "Can you do one more flight?"

"I." Gasp. "Think." Gasp. "So."

"Then go." He pushed me ahead of him, and I tumbled out of the door and landed on all fours in the hallway.

Slowly, air came back to my lungs. What had happened? How had it sucked all the air from the stairwell? No, it had somehow fooled my lungs into thinking it had.

The door opened, and I staggered to my feet. Sir Raleigh, back in cat form, darted into the hallway. He ran for my and Lawrence's room and left bloody paw prints behind him. Just before the door closed, Ellerin waved and disappeared.

"Sir Raleigh!" I followed the grimalkin, holding on to the wall for support since standing made me dizzy.

Lawrence opened the door, and I fell into his arms. He steadied me, but I pushed him away.

"Attend to the cat. Sir Raleigh is hurt."

Something bumped into the wards around the room, and the external walls shimmered with silver light for a second.

"It's trying to get in," Lawrence said.

"I can see that." Now that I could breathe, I could think. "What do you want, Monster?" I yelled through the door.

Sibilant laughter echoed around us. *"Wouldn't you like to know?"*

"Yes, actually, I would."

"You'll find out soon enough." The walls shimmered again, and the wards almost cracked. I placed my hands on the wall and poured what strength I had into the security spells.

One more hit from the soul-eater, and they held, although I knew it grew stronger, so this solution wouldn't last forever. Plus, I couldn't hide in a hotel room indefinitely.

"Are you all right?" Lawrence asked.

I opened my mouth to croak out, "I don't think so." Then I collapsed, and the world went black.

11

LAWRENCE

I picked Reine up from the floor and placed her on the bed. I shouldn't have been able to see the spells, but I had. A sign of the bond we'd started to develop? She had run to me, after all. Or to the warded room? It didn't matter. I stroked a tousled white curl from her forehead and allowed myself a brief caress along her cheek.

Once I ensured she slept, I turned my attention to Sir Raleigh, who licked his wounds.

"And what happened to you?" I asked. He allowed me to pick him up and place him on a towel on the desk. He looked like he'd been in a fight with another cat, and he swatted my hand away when I tried to clean the lacerations. To my amazement, they seemed better when I re-examined him. He continued to clean himself, and finally, all the cuts had closed. He wouldn't even have any scars.

"Well, then, looks like you can take care of yourself."

He purred and shoved himself under my hand for a quick caress, then jumped up on the bed where Reine lay. She watched me through half-lidded eyes.

"How is he?" she asked.

"Great. Not only is your cat self-cleaning, he's self-healing. What happened?"

"Soul-eater ambushed me on Rhys' floor while I waited for the elevator."

I went cold and stifled a growl. I knew I shouldn't have left her alone, but I'd trusted her brother to bring her back up. Of course he hadn't. That's what I got for trusting a Fae.

"You're angry," she said and rose to her elbows. I helped her sit.

"Yes, I'm angry. I should have gone with you, waited while you talked to Rhys. Then I could have guarded you."

She started to argue, then shook her head. "I had help. I had Sir Raleigh."

I sensed she held back, but I didn't want to push. Her wide-eyed gaze flicked around the room, and she held her bottom lip between her teeth. That she appeared so fragile and scared made my temper flare further. "You should have had Rhys. He knows what we're up against. Why didn't he at least walk you up? Did he even offer?"

"No." She shook her head and let out a rueful chuckle. "He had a hot date coming up."

"What?" I stood and paced. "We're fighting for your life, and he's fucking 'Con-goers?'"

"Lawrence!"

I stopped and folded my arms. She looked up at me, her eyes wide.

"What?"

"I've never heard you swear."

"I didn't swear. I used a verb."

"A dirty verb." Now she genuinely laughed, and the sound calmed me. "Come sit."

I complied, but I didn't settle in close enough to touch her. My body still tingled from the after-effects of that dance, and that, combined with my protective instinct's frustration at failing her again, made me want to clutch her close and do the things both the man and the gargoyle in me desired.

"What do you have against Rhys?" Reine asked.

"Besides his complete incompetence at accomplishing what he's supposed to be doing? Failing to try?"

"He's trying—"

"I'll say."

She shot me a *shut up* look, and I took a deep breath, willing my irritability to subside. Normally it would obey me—and come back as a case of reflux that challenged my stomach of stone later—but it still simmered below the surface and demanded to be acknowledged.

"Yes, he's definitely trying in that sense, too, but surely you've encountered people—creatures—who weren't very good at their jobs. What do you typically do?"

"Fire them and move on, but I can't fire your brother."

"No, as much as I wish you could." She rubbed her temples. "I don't know what my mother was thinking. Probably trying to sneak him in on my redemption."

"Your what?" This was new. "I thought you were here to help figure out who leaked the CLS vector."

"I was. It's a condition for a Faerie task I must complete. So is containing the soul-eater."

A bunch of thoughts hit my brain at once. How did a Fae get caught up in a Faerie task? She should be smarter than that. Also, what would she get if she completed it? My gut told me I wouldn't like the answer. I snapped into scientist mode—I needed all the facts. "Start at the beginning and tell me every-thing. There could be information in there that would help with the soul-eater's capture."

"I will on one condition."

"Oh?" I allowed my lips to form a small grin. What would she ask for—another kiss? Another dance? Something more?

I didn't expect her answer.

"You're going to tell me why you hate Fae so much. I see now it goes beyond the traditional enmity between our people since the rift you mentioned. It's personal for you."

I thought for a second, then nodded. "All right. My deepest darkest secret for yours. You first."

12

———

REINE

I didn't want to tell Lawrence about what had happened to get me exiled, but I had no choice. Or I felt I didn't. He had to understand why I protected Rhys, why our fates were tied together and why my mother had sent Rhys, although I didn't know with any certainty myself.

"It started at the Battle of Culloden." If I closed my eyes and delved into my memory, I could still hear the sounds of the battle, smell the smoke and the blood. And, closer by, the terrible grunt and moan of a man being bayoneted. That had happened too often that day.

"What were you doing there?" Lawrence asked and brought me back from the slaughter.

"My grandmother had tasked me and Rhys to go see what was happening and to confirm that a vargamore—a half-wizard, half-werewolf creature—was attempting to interfere with humanity. This particular one hated werewolves, and since many of them fought for the Scots, the vargamore allied with the English. I don't know what my grandmother was thinking. Perhaps she wanted to see if there would be a chance of an alliance."

"With such an awful creature?"

"Yes. You know the Fae are ruthless and lack moral scruples. If it would be to our advantage, my grandmother would ally with the devil himself."

"So, you were spying on the battle. What went wrong?"

Frustration and worry flooded through me at the memory. "My grandmother, and then my mother, had warned us to stay together and not stray too far from the standing stones that hid the fairy circle that formed our portal into Faerie. But when we saw just how big the battle was, we agreed to split up to get more intel. It was Rhys' idea, and I should have argued more, but I was eager for the chance to have a few hours to myself away from my brother." I shook my head. "Apparently, I can't ever escape my responsibility for him."

"What do you mean?"

"Ever since he'd been born, my mother had tasked me with taking care of him. I was always more a mother to him than she was."

"You let him do something independently, which made you a more effective parental figure."

Sir Raleigh crawled on to my lap, and I stroked his fur as he purred. "Fae don't parent like other beings, but thanks. Perhaps acting like a human made sense, but it backfired."

"His scar," Lawrence guessed.

"Yes. He ran into some trouble. Someone insulted him, a fight ensued, and a Templar cut Rhys' face with a blessed blade, which left a scar. I tried to heal it, but..." I closed my eyes, and Sir Raleigh pushed his head under one of my hands. The cries of the wounded cells had seared themselves into my memory, and not even the cat's comfort could erase them or my sense of guilt and regret.

"It wasn't your fault, Reine." Lawrence rubbed my back again, and I took comfort in the gesture. The combination of him and the cat worked better for me than Xanax.

"But it was. If I hadn't let him go off on his own. If I'd listened to my mother..." I'd still be in Faerie, and I wouldn't have a sweet grimalkin on my lap or a gargoyle with broad shoulders to lean my head against, which I did.

"You wouldn't have been exiled," he finished. "They punished you for his actions? Can he still go home?"

"No." I straightened, although I could have allowed myself to be supported by him. The detergent in his clothes and his own unique scent of sun-warmed marble with a chocolate-like hint of soil mixed in my nose. Since when had I enjoyed gargoyle smell?

Since I'd met this one.

"No," I started again, willing myself not to be distracted by our closeness. This had been the first time something had been able to pull me from the memory of the great injustice that had been done to me. "Fae rulers have never allowed imperfect Fae to reside in Faerie, at least not in the Light Court. I don't know about the dark or gray, so Rhys can't go back."

"I see. I thought there would be a gargoyle in the story from his and your reactions to me."

"I'm sorry. I was rude when we first met, wasn't I?"

He smiled and put his arm around me. "And I was an insufferable prick convinced I knew everything important about you."

"That is very true."

"But I need to know, did a gargoyle have something to do with what happened to your brother? You said a Templar. I thought they had been massacred and died out by that time?"

"They had, but a few pockets survived, and even after they dwindled, certain orders would use their costume, counting on the fact that people would make the association with Templar principles whether they espoused them or not." I found myself not wanting to mention the gargoyle, but I had to. "And the man who cut Rhys was assisted by a gargoyle, who kept Rhys from being able to dodge the blade. That's why he hates you."

"I can't say I blame him." Lawrence's torso heaved with a sigh against my side. "And I understand why you protect him. You're lucky to still have family, even if it's imperfect."

I stilled, afraid to move and startle him away from a subject he'd avoided—his past. I knew so little of him, not even his age. "You said you were going to tell me something." I spoke carefully so I wouldn't spook him. "Why you have an issue with Fae."

"Right. And it ties in to why I don't have family."

AT THAT MOMENT, my stomach growled. Lawrence laughed and suggested we order dinner. Once we'd eaten and sat across from each other at the small table room service had wheeled in, I poured more wine into Lawrence's glass from the bottle of Chablis we'd agreed to share. I also dimmed the lights to give the room a more intimate air, and candlelight made shadows dance across the walls.

"Tell me all your secrets," I said in my most sultry voice.

One corner of his mouth turned up in a rakish half-grin. "And what will you give me for them?"

"I shall give you...a kiss." I held my breath.

"And do I get a deposit?"

I stood, walked around the table, and pecked him on one of his chiseled cheekbones. "How's that?"

"I suppose it will have to do. I expect more later." He drew his brows together and studied his wine, which he slowly swirled.

"You don't have to if you don't feel like it," I told him and immediately regretted it. Again, that feeling of treading on fragile ground made me wish I had some idea of what to expect. I could understand his hesitation—I hadn't wanted to mention the gargoyle's part in Rhys' maiming for fear it would ruin the uneasy peace between us. But I also wanted to know who, truly, was Lawrence Gordon, gargoyle and veterinarian... and intriguing, sexy man?

"We'll see," was his noncommittal reply.

Challenge or rejection? I took a quick sip of wine to quell the sting. How had our flirtation gone sour so quickly?

His next words told me—he'd gotten sucked into the past. "So, you want to know why I have a prejudice against Fae that goes beyond the rift in our history..." He inhaled deeply. "My childhood was a happy one until I was the age that has a human equivalent of seven or eight. We lived in a cottage in the woods near what is now the outskirts of Newcastle. It was all forest and farmland at the time."

I did some mental calculations against what little I knew of English city development. Newcastle was a fairly populous city, but it had maintained parks around it.

"What did your parents do?"

"Mum raised me. Da worked on the ships in Sandgate."

That would potentially make him about four hundred, since Newcastle had been a busy shipbuilding hub starting in the 1600s.

He continued to gaze into his wine, and I wondered what he saw. A small boy watching his father work on building ships? It would be good work for a gargoyle since one of their elements was water. They often lived near rivers, places where earth and water coexisted.

"What happened?" I asked softly to give him the option to ignore the question, although I hoped he wouldn't.

"One day there was an argument at the docks. Da came home disturbed and told Mum to make sure the doors were locked." He roughened his deep voice, and his accent went from neutral to thick Northeastern English, which sounded like

Scottish Light. "'Although it may not be enough to keep the devil out.' It was a tense evening. Da kept peeking out of the window. 'Who are ye lookin' for?' Mum would ask, although she knew. She wanted to make him talk, to say more about what happened. I half-wanted to see the man since I'd not ever seen a real devil before." He shook his head. "The innocence of childhood. I remember that desire because it was the last childish one I had."

He again lapsed into silence. The shadows from the candle-light played across his face like those of clouds across fields in a sped-up landscape film. I waited, tense, and the image of the cottage and Rhys pulling his hood over his face flashed into my mind. I went cold when Lawrence continued.

"There were three of them."

I almost slumped in relief. I had only seen Rhys in my vision, so it couldn't have been the same scenario.

Lawrence continued, his tone rote. "I couldn't see their faces, but the way they moved... I knew they were Fae. They wore scarves and hoods so all I could see were their eyes, dark with rage and hate. They broke down the door, knocked my mother aside like she was no more than a nuisance, and..." He closed his eyes. "I ran at one of them, and when my father lunged for me, that's when the one with the blade made his move. He killed my father, and I couldn't do anything." With a crack, the stem of his wineglass shattered, and he jumped back, then stuck his left thumb in his mouth. I heard the song of his blood then, and it sang of centuries-deep pain and the need to hide any vulnerability from a world that wouldn't hesitate to take whatever was most precious from him.

"Here," I said. "Let me."

"No, I'll be fine. I need to clean it."

He went into the bathroom, and I carefully gathered the glass I could find. It wouldn't cut me, I knew, but I still handled each piece gently. It had been broken out of pain, had responded in kind, and I whispered to it so it wouldn't hurt anyone else and the pain-for-pain pattern would end.

By the time Lawrence emerged, I had cleaned the mess and put the table in the hall to be collected along with a note of apology and warning about the broken glass. He'd wrapped his thumb in a washcloth, which he held tightly against it.

"How bad is it?" I asked.

"Not too bad. I may need stitches, though."

I placed my hand over his makeshift bandage. "May I heal you?"

He turned away, but not before I saw the revolted expression.

"No," he said. "You need to save your strength. I'll be fine."

I stepped back, stung, and drew my hand back from his. "Don't lie to me. You don't want to be touched by Fae magic."

"Do you blame me?" His wistful tone softened the question, but I still crossed my arms over the turmoil brewing around my heart.

"No, I suppose not. Not after what you just told me." I refrained from pointing out he'd responded well when we danced. That had been different, though. Or had it? I hadn't asked his permission, which was typical Fae. Had that been what angered him at the club? But then he'd kissed me.

"And you do need to conserve your energy. We'll drive over to Stone Mountain in the morning, charge you up. Meanwhile, I'm going to bed. It's been a very long day."

"All right, good night." I wanted to take his hand and sneak in some healing, but he hadn't wanted it, and I couldn't force him. No one made a gargoyle do anything it didn't want to.

He retreated to his room and closed the door. I sat on the bed and petted Sir Raleigh, who rubbed against me. My heart ached for the little boy who had lost his father and...

Wait, he hadn't said anything about his mother. Had she been killed, too?

I knocked on the door.

"Yes?" he asked and opened it.

"I'm sorry, but you didn't finish your story. What happened to your mum?"

He rubbed his eyes. "We fled, went into hiding. We didn't know if the Fae would eventually come after us, too."

"Do you remember if they said why they were going after your father? That seems extreme after an argument."

"Yes, but they never got specific. Only that he looked like someone who had wronged one of them, had stolen something precious." He squeezed his injured hand and winced. "Apparently they didn't know the difference between gargoyle and dragon shifters."

"Right, good, thanks." All right, it couldn't have been Rhys. He enjoyed luxury but wouldn't resort to murder over a stolen bauble.

"Anything else, Doctor River?"

The words, *"You never collected your kiss"* hovered on my tongue, but I couldn't make them emerge. The moment had passed. "No, Doctor Gordon, that is all. Sleep well."

I suspected neither of us would.

13

———

LAWRENCE

The bitter irony of Reine's and my story exchange was that I simultaneously felt more connected to her and fearful of what would result from our revelations. Well, besides a sore thumb.

Reine's sorrow, disappointment, and anxiety floated through the air, and the electric sensations dissipated as she drifted to sleep. She thought she was a clever Fae, but I'd seen her expression grow guarded as I described the Fae attack on my family. Could she know something about what happened?

Ted's words about the answer to an old puzzle coming along with more pain than I could imagine floated through my head. But then she'd looked relieved when I said there were three of them. She'd seen something, perhaps that morning before the witch-hunt spell when she'd been warming up the bowl for Aria. The vision had freaked her out. Not that Fae freak-outs were similar to human ones. With the Fae, they happened internally. Humans acted out, Fae acted in, which made them all the more ruthless when it was time to take revenge and transfer that pain to others.

Well, gargoyles could be ruthless, too. That's why I refused to live among them in caves and crags deep in the hills and mountains. Persecuted races had nothing to lose when they perceived attacks.

I felt Reine's transition to true slumber, a curtain falling on the drama of the day, and the theatre taking an intermission before the next act. My thumb had mostly stopped bleeding, and I wrapped it with some gauze and tape, but I knew I'd want something less bulky for the following day.

All right, I needed to get away.

Sir Raleigh popped into the spot beside me, and the air he disturbed flowed over me in a cool blast.

"Where have you been?" I asked. He looked back at me with eyes more intelligent and cunning than a typical cat's, which had cleverness enough to spare. "And who have you been talking to?"

He turned around and curled up beside me, purring. He even turned his belly up toward me, and I couldn't resist petting the soft fur with my uninjured hand.

"You can try to charm me, but I know you're up to something."

He licked his one white paw and started to wash his face. I had to give it to him—he was ridiculously cute. Well, unless he turned into his bat-winged panther form, but I supposed we had that in common.

"I'm going to see if someone downstairs can float me a Band-Aid," I told him. Not that I needed to report to him what I was going to do, but it felt nice to talk to someone or something that didn't want anything from me.

Or did he? The ways of cats, especially cats that weren't cats, were mysterious.

He paused and glanced up at me questioningly, then went back to his cleaning.

"Keep an eye on her for me, will you?"

Although felines had a limited number of muscles in their

faces, their eyes expressed volumes. In this case, only one word came to mind with the glare he gave me, *"Duh."*

"Okay, then, get in there." I stood and walked to the door, which I opened a crack.

Now his expression said, *"Really? You want me to walk in there?"*

"Yes. Don't wake her up by teleporting next to her and chilling her."

He stood, arched into a stretch, then jumped off the bed and sauntered into the other room like he thought it was his idea.

I shook my head and closed the door. What was he, really? He definitely had the cattitude down.

I put my key card in one hip pocket, phone in the other, and wallet in my back pocket. When I slipped into the hallway, careful to close the door quietly, I found it deserted. Some of the rooms I passed emanated sounds of conversations and music—room parties or gatherings of friends who hadn't seen each other since the last fantasy convention, some not since the last Fae-Con.

I stifled a growl, not because I begrudged them their good time, but because I tired of being the gargoyle on the outside.

The elevator took me downstairs without any stops, and I hoped the lobby would be quiet. As before, the farther I went away from Reine, the more I felt I needed to be there protecting her. Thankfully, Sir Raleigh—whatever his other agenda— seemed determined to watch over her. I reminded myself he could be fierce when needed even if he hadn't fared well earlier. But if something happened in the room, someone would let me know. Hell, I'd feel it before anyone could reach out.

Only one person was on duty at the front desk, a young African-American woman with short hair and beautiful hazel eyes. She wrinkled her nose as I approached, but sounded friendly when she asked, "Can I help you, Sir?"

I made sure to speak as clearly and non-drunkenly as possible. "Yes, I had an accident earlier. Broke a wineglass, spilled it on myself, and cut my thumb. Do you happen to have any Band-Aids?"

She relaxed slightly. No doubt she'd been fearing a belligerent drunk guest. That was the dark side of Cons—always one or two jerks at one this size who thought they could push hotel staff around.

"We don't have any here, but there's a First-Aid kit for sale in our concierge shop." She named an outlandish price for something that probably contained three Band-Aids, a small packet of antibiotic ointment, and an alcohol wipe.

"Thanks, I'll keep searching." All right, I could have afforded it without any problem, but my father had always been thrifty, and tonight the ghost of his memory floated close to my shoulder.

I wandered to the main 'Con hall and found the two night staff people on duty. Samir was nowhere to be found, but a lovely woman with long black hair and dark eyes smiled at me when I approached.

"I'm Inala," she said, her accent slightly British like Samir's. "Do you need something?"

I made the same request to her, and she nodded to her companion, a twenty-something-year-old girl with curly red hair and freckles. "Corali will help you."

"Accidents always happen," Corali agreed and dug through an opaque plastic storage box. "Seems like more today than previously. I'll run out tomorrow and grab more, Inala."

"Thank you."

I looked more closely and saw Inala's eyes were shadowed by dark circles. I accepted the two Band-Aids Corali gave me and thanked her, then asked, "What do you mean by more accidents today?"

Inala rubbed her eyes. "There's something weird about this

'Con. People have been particularly clumsy. It's like they space out and run into things, trip over each other, drop things..."

"Breakable things," Corali added. "And drinks. So many spilled drinks."

"Is that why y'all are hanging out here? I didn't expect to find anyone back here, but I'm glad you are."

Inala sighed. "Yes. Normally we don't staff the desk at night, but we decided it would be wise to not leave the hotel staff to handle things. We don't want them kicking the 'Con out next year for being too much trouble. Or raising the prices for the convention space and rooms."

I had no doubt Jimmy Leak would do that if he felt the 'Con was more trouble than it was worth. I also guessed who, or what, was responsible for the accidents.

"Well, thanks again. I'll try to be more careful." I turned to go, but Inala leaned over and put a hand on my arm.

"Wait," she said. "Do you know something? Samir told me about a group of people who were doing some sort of role-playing thing, and who seemed very serious about it."

"Yes. We're not playing a game. Something is here and is stalking your convention."

"What sort of something?"

I opened my mouth to tell her, but icy fingers closed around my throat. "Do not tell her anything," a voice hissed in my ear.

"Can't say. Thanks again," I choked out and walked away, the feeling of the soul-eater clinging to me, its hands or tendrils or something around my throat. Once I reached a quiet place, I unleashed my inner gargoyle and didn't change, but the energy managed to push the soul-eater off me.

"What do you want?" I asked.

Cold air swirled around me, and it whispered, "Freedom."

"From what?"

A rasping chuckle. "Tell your girlfriend I'm coming for her, and you won't be able to protect her. No one will."

"Why do you want her? Can you take me instead?"

More laughter, then, "Tell her, tell her, tell her..."

I resisted the urge to garg out. That would cause too many questions, and my instincts told me the soul-eater had gone.

I thought through what I had learned and next steps as I went back up to our joined rooms. First, the creature was toying with the humans in the hotel. Or perhaps practicing its possession skills so as to master subtle or—I shivered at the thought—undetectable takeovers so it could get close to Reine when it was time to do whatever it wanted to with her.

That decided me. We were going to take a sunrise walk at Stone Mountain the next morning so she could be at full strength.

Second, someone had given Reine knowledge of the soul-eater earlier that week, a Fae named Troubadour. We needed to talk to him again, as much as I hated bringing yet another Fae into the situation.

Third, the soul-eater was growing in strength and in more control of its effects on others. It had been able to attack me without possessing me. Was that because it had taken me over before?

Great, yet another Fae creature I had a connection to. I apologized to my father—this certainly had not been the life I'd intended. Nor had I ever planned to start falling for a Fae. But when I returned to our joined rooms, the first thing I did was check on her. She lay on the bed, her white curls spread out around her, and Sir Raleigh curled up next to her. Gods, she was beautiful, although even in slumber, she didn't appear innocent. No Fae could.

I sat on my bed and put my head in my hands. Instead of clearing my head, my excursion had only led to more questions, the foremost of which was, could I link my fate to hers and risk the pain Ted had foretold? And was it already too late to not do so?

I woke the next morning to a soft paw batting at my nose. Then, when I turned over, the cat jumped over my head, landing with a *pouf!* on the pillow. He licked me between the eyes.

"Aaaugh!" I bolted upright and rubbed my face, wincing when I recalled my thumb injury. Sir Raleigh cocked his head at me as if to say, *"About time you got up."*

"What is it?" I checked the clock—5:45 in the morning. "Why are you waking me? Are you out of food?"

He jumped down from the bed and padded to the door between my and Reine's rooms, then turned to look at me.

"You want me to follow. All right." I threw on a robe and walked into the Fae's room. The scents from our dinner the night before still lingered in the air, and she lay in the same position I'd seen her last night, hair spread over her pillow, and one arm across her stomach. The stillness and quiet pressed in on me, and with a jolt, I saw—or didn't see, rather—breathing. Her hand on her stomach rose and fell once, then stilled again.

"Reine?" I knelt on the bed beside her and caressed her cheek. "Reine, wake up."

Sir Raleigh leaped onto her pillow and licked her in the same place he'd gotten me. No response. Just another single breath.

"What's going on with her?" I asked and cursed my lack of knowledge about the Fae. I'd heard that when away from the source of their power for too long, certain magical creatures went into a sort of low-power mode. Could this be it? It helped her to conserve her energy, but...

"We need to get her out of here, to Stone Mountain. She needs to recharge."

I'd never seen a cat nod before, but Sir Raleigh did.

"Glad you agree, but we have a problem."

Another head tilt.

"The soul-eater is out there. If it gets to her like this, it could take her. She needs strength to fight it."

An image flashed into my mind of me covering her with a sheet and carrying her out, hiding her.

"No, then everyone will think I killed her."

A count of eleven between breaths this time. Had it been ten before? How long could she last in this strange stasis?

With a non-feline sigh, Sir Raleigh stalked over to the night-stand and knocked Reine's phone to the floor.

"Now you decide to be a cat?"

He pointedly looked at the phone, and when I picked it up, an image of a small black and white bird with sharp beak came to mind. A kestrel.

Call Kestrel. Right, the grimalkin was thinking better than I was. Apparently, Fae creatures didn't need coffee. Kestrel was having a flare of deception power. That could be useful. "If she's still having her magic surge. I'll try."

Kestrel sounded alert when she answered the phone, and when I apologized for waking her said, "I was already awake. Have been for an hour. What's up, Uncle Lawrence?"

I explained the situation to her, and she said she'd be on her way. In the fifteen minutes it took her to get there, I threw on some clothes, did a rudimentary morning wash-up and teeth brush, and spent the rest of the time sitting on Reine's bed, holding her hand and counting the time between breaths. The gap had reached twenty seconds when a soft knock came at the door.

I opened the door to see Corey, but then the image wavered, and it was Kestrel. Her wide grin vanished when she saw Reine.

"You're still having the flare. Good."

She wiped sweat from her temple. "It's trying to slip away, and something else is coming through. Let's hurry."

We got Reine out of bed and put some shoes on her—she'd

need them for her walk down the mountain. I'd figure out how to get her up it when we got there. Kestrel and I supported her between us, and our difference in height made it awkward, but we managed.

"What are you projecting?" I asked.

"Two college-aged people supporting a friend who'd had too much to drink. Sir Raleigh, you're on your own."

With another decidedly un-catlike nod, the cat vanished.

We made it down the hall and into the elevator, where we both agreed without speaking to lean against the side. Who knew Fae could be so heavy?

Twenty-five seconds between breaths. Were her lips turning blue? Hard to tell in the dim lighting.

When we reached the lobby, a surprise waited for us. A familiar-looking man in a gray suit and hat that came straight out of the sixties met us.

"Here, I'll help you."

Both Kestrel and I were sweating, me because I held most of Reine's weight—this was the longest I'd transported her—and Kestrel with the effort of keeping up the projection. Neither of us had the strength to protest when he took Reine and lifted her easily, her head lolling. I gathered her soft curls so they wouldn't drag on the ground. I'd imagined running my hands through her hair, but I wasn't prepared for the softness and feeling of life in them.

"When she's at home in her full power, sometimes people with extra sight see creatures in her hair," the man said without effort in spite of carrying her.

"Who are you, sir?" I asked.

He shook his head. "Not here. I'll tell you in a moment."

Sir Raleigh appeared on my shoulder with another wave of cold air. Had he gone for help, or something else? How had the mysterious stranger known we needed him?

We followed the man in the gray suit outside to a waiting

top-end Tesla. He put Reine in the passenger seat, and I let her hair slip through my fingers as he arranged her. My stomach clenched. Would I have the chance to do so in a sensual way? Or were we too late?

Thirty seconds, and there was definitely a purplish tint to her nails.

Kestrel and I climbed into the backseat. He dialed Stone Mountain into his GPS, and we were on our way.

"What happened?" he asked when he paused at a light, and the glare he gave me in the rearview mirror made me feel all of about five years old. Sorrow welled up within me—no one had given me a stern paternal look since my own father, and after telling Reine my story, the grief lay close to the surface.

"I don't know. We were both asleep, and Sir Raleigh woke me." The cat had returned to Reine and lay curled up in her lap. I could hear his purring from the backseat.

"She's been traveling to Faerie in her dreams," he said. "I don't know how. Something must have attacked her there."

"The soul-eater?" I asked.

"No, it's firmly fixed in this realm. Something else."

Kestrel had gone pale, and when I touched her hand, it was clammy.

"Kestrel, are you all right?"

"I don't know, Uncle Lawrence. I was fine until..." She inclined her head toward the man in gray. "The deception power is gone, but something is trying to come through, something strong."

"Don't fight it," the stranger said. "It could be useful."

"If I don't fight it, it will take over! This one's...different."

"Who are you to tell her what to do?" I snapped. "She's struggled with this enough."

"Someone who knows a thing or two about paranormal powers. And as for who I am, you can call me the Gray Fae."

Whispered conversations from my childhood came back to

me then, the old women at family gatherings gossiping about other creatures. "Are you truly one of the gray?"

"I am not truly of anything, Gargoyle. But then, you aren't either, are you?"

Reine took a deep breath, and the sound rasped.

"What's happening to her?"

"She's overextended herself, and the soul-eater has weakened her. It takes more from her with each attack." His grim tone made my heart sink. "It shouldn't be able to, even with her so far away from home. There's more at play here than just a dark Fae creature and a Fae princess."

"What do you think it is?"

He shook his head. "One must never accuse unless one has more than sufficient evidence."

I remembered, then, where I'd seen him. "You were at Ashlee Wyatt's club the first time we visited. On the stairs. You were going up as we were coming out of the upstairs VIP area." Uncertainty crept in. "Are you working for her?"

He laughed, a mocking sound. "No, I don't work for anyone, Sir Gargoyle. Never forget that."

"I'm not Sir anything," I grumbled.

"Not as far as you know."

With that cryptic statement, he pulled into the park, and the rangers waved him through. My ears buzzed, and I recognized that he used some sort of glamour.

Kestrel sat doubled over with clenched fists pressed to her chest, and I touched her shoulder. Now she burned hot.

"We need to get help for her."

"Again, stop fighting," the man snapped. "What do you feel?"

"Voices, so many voices," she whispered. "It's medium power. But it's letting all of them in."

When he pulled into the parking lot by the gondola station, Reine stirred. Her nails returned to their normal color.

"Being close to the mountain is already helping," I said.

"The granite runs through the area. She'll get the most benefit on the top if we can catch the sunrise. Hurry."

"Kestrel, can you walk?" I asked.

When she straightened, I drew back. Her eyes had gone bright golden yellow. "Yes, we can walk," she said in a resonant voice.

"Something's possessed her! Kestrel, sweetie, come back."

"One problem at a time," the gray Fae snapped. "We'll address it at the top. Come on!"

14

REINE

The darkness that had a hold on me faded and I took a deep breath, then another. The blackness turned midnight blue, then lightened through all the shades of blue to purple, pink, and finally I opened my eyes to see the sun peeking over the horizon of the granite monolith. I lay on my side, my head cradled on a strong thigh, and someone stroked my hair. Sir Raleigh lay across my waist, and I lifted a hand to scratch him behind the ears.

As the sun rose, golden light spread through my veins, renewing my fire, and my earth energies rooted me into the granite beneath me, pulling the strength of the mountain into my spirit. I closed my eyes involuntarily as the breeze whispered around me and stirred my hair, lifting my curls with the morning humidity—air and water. That only left one element, and I moved my hand from Sir Raleigh to Lawrence's leg beneath my head. Our connection pulsed through me, and I felt to my core that as much as I didn't want to hurt him, he would miss me when I returned home to Faerie.

And, worse, I would miss him.

"What happened?" I asked and straightened to sitting, my weight supported by my shaky left arm.

"We were hoping you could tell us," Lawrence said. "He said you'd been attacked in Faerie, where you've been going in your dreams."

I scrunched my forehead, trying to remember. "I don't recall any dreams last night, but that doesn't mean I haven't had any." Great, if sleeping wasn't safe, I had no way to restore myself outside of trips to Stone Mountain, which was a twenty-minute drive during a light traffic time, and I was coming to find that Atlanta didn't have many light traffic times.

"You have been visiting Faerie," Kestrel asserted, but not in her voice.

"Troubadour?" I asked. "What are you doing here? Is he who told you I've been visiting Faerie?"

"No, it was..." Lawrence looked around. "He's gone."

"The Gray Fae does not stay for the difficult conversations," Troubadour said through Kestrel and spread her features into a male sneer.

"The Gray..." Ellerin. It had to have been him. But why? "And what are you doing here? Lawrence, please help me up."

Lawrence stood, then pulled me to my feet.

"Can you bring her back?" he whispered.

"I think so. Troubadour, what made you come through this morning?"

"I saw a doorway open. This one is an interesting body." He wiggled Kestrel's fingers. "I could get used to this."

"Don't you dare!" Lawrence said and started forward. I grabbed his upper arm.

"He won't." A different energy, one I'd come to believe I'd never feel again, spread through me, straightened my spine, and lifted my chin. My Fae princess authority burned through me, and I knew I could command him.

Troubadour's grin vanished, and Kestrel's eyes widened. "I bring you a warning, Princess."

"At what price?" I asked before he could continue and trap me in an accidental Fae bargain.

"Again, no price, Princess. Just remember me when you return to Faerie."

"When you...?" Lawrence asked.

"Later." That was definitely a conversation I didn't want to have right then.

Troubadour continued, "While a dark Fae summoned the soul-eater, a light Fae released it into the world. That's how it has so much influence and why it's so dangerous to you."

"I knew that."

He inclined Kestrel's head. "But what you don't know is that this plot goes all the way up to your grandmother's court."

"Not just the capital." I tapped my lip with my right index finger. "That makes perfect, horrible sense. How do you know so much?"

"Because I'm the dark Fae who released it." Kestrel slumped forward, and Lawrence rushed to catch her.

"Wait!" But it was too late. "Hades! He knew all along." But why would a dark Fae be helping me, especially since he released something to hurt me?

Plots within plots within plots... but that meant Troubadour had either been deceived and betrayed by whoever he worked with, or he had developed a conscience. My money would be on the former. But he was still too frightened of whoever he worked with to go against them directly.

"Some help here?" Lawrence asked. I knelt by Kestrel and put my hand on her clammy forehead.

"She's having a flare of medium magic," I said. "It's a strong one. And she can't control whatever's coming through."

Kestrel opened her eyes, and this time when she spoke, the cadence and accent were achingly familiar, although the voice was her own. "Be careful, child." Then her eyes rolled back in her head, and she passed out again.

"Who was that?" Lawrence asked.

"My grandmother. Hold her still." I placed my index fingers at Kestrel's temples and my thumbs at her jawline just below her molars. With the energy of the mountain backing me, I closed the doorway in her mind that the flare of medium power had opened.

"What are you doing?"

"Closing the door for now. She's had too much hurt and grief and can't control it."

"Will she be able to open it again?"

"She should be, in the right circumstances, but she needs to get her emotions under control first. By the time she can, it will have likely faded on its own."

Kestrel's eyelids fluttered open, and this time, only she looked back at us.

"What happened?" she asked. "Reine, are you all right?"

Her concern touched my heart more than I expected. "Yes, I'm fine. You all got me here just in time. You had a flare of medium power. Do you remember?"

"Y-yes. It felt like I cracked inside, and all the voices came through. I fought it, but I couldn't control it."

"The gray Fae wanted Troubadour to come through," Lawrence said. "He kept telling you not to fight it. Do you remember him?"

"Vaguely. It all feels like a dream."

Speaking of dreams, I needed to know what I'd been dreaming about, how I'd been attacked, but I didn't know how.

Well, there was one possibility.

"Kestrel, love, I know this is a lot to ask, but can you get in touch with Aria for me?"

～

RHYS' text came through as we rode down the mountain in the gondola. Kestrel and I both felt too shaky to walk, although I wouldn't have minded more contact with the energies of the monolith. I didn't feel like being nice to Rhys. So far he hadn't turned out to be much help aside from bringing me tea once.

"Hey, sis, where are you?"

I sent him a short answer. *"Out."*

"We need to talk," was his reply.

"About?"

"Nightmares."

That got my attention. "Kestrel, what's the address of Aria's shop? I need to have Rhys meet us there."

He must have driven Fae-fast since he got there at the same time we did. When we arrived, Aria flipped the door sign to *Closed* and brought us to her back room. This time she had warm American biscuits on the sideboard along with an assortment of jams waiting for us.

"Figured you hadn't eaten breakfast yet," she said. "It's all organic, mostly local. Is this okay for your Fae stomachs?"

My Fae stomach growled in response, and everyone laughed.

Aria grinned. "I'll take that as a yes. Y'all help yourselves."

I ate and recharged my physical body as Kestrel and Lawrence filled Aria and Rhys in on what had happened that morning.

"I had nightmares, too," Rhys said and narrowed his eyes at Lawrence, who paused his precise biscuit-buttering and jamming procedure to glare back.

"What?" Lawrence asked.

"You were in them, mate. Did you have something to do with them?" Although he must have sounded purely belligerent to the humans, Rhys' tone had an edge of fear.

"What did you dream?" I asked.

"That's personal. That's why I only wanted to talk to *you*, not your entourage."

A chuckle slipped out. Yes, it seemed I traveled with an entourage these days. "Well, it is befitting of a Fae princess to have her attendants." And for some reason, I felt more the princess today than I had in a while. Something about the conversation with Troubadour, as disturbing as it was, had released a part of me I'd locked away after my exile. And it had been so long ago I'd forgotten where I'd put it or even that I had it.

What else did I need to clean out of my mental storage? A lot had likely accumulated in my five centuries of life.

Fae didn't do therapy. There had to be another way.

"I'm not an attendant," Lawrence grumbled, bringing me out of my thoughts. I didn't mind. It frightened me to think what else I could have forgotten about myself. There surely had to be not-so-good parts as well as the ones I didn't know I longed for. I envied the humans with their stubborn tendencies to focus on the future.

"You're not a consort, either, mate."

"Rhys!" My entire face heated. Not that we'd done anything to make Lawrence a consort, but that didn't mean I hated the idea. The feel of his muscular thigh under my head and hands that morning came to mind, and I was sure the flush in my cheeks deepened.

Lawrence spoke coolly. "Your sister's and my relationship is our business, not yours. I didn't see you rushing to help her this morning."

Ha. Touché, bratty little brother.

Rhys scowled, but he didn't argue further. That disturbed me—he'd never been one to back down from a fight or take it to an extreme conclusion.

Aria cleared her throat. "Well, if everyone's had enough to eat, we can proceed. Princess, since you and my black quartz bowl seem to have a good rapport, I thought we'd try that again."

"Works for me." I slid a glance at Rhys, who responded with a brief arch of his eyebrow, which in our secret sibling language, meant, *Don't say too much.*

I dipped my chin—*Understood.*

Aria brought out the bowl and set it in front of me. She murmured something as she filled it with water from a crystal pitcher, and even before the water stilled, images began to swirl on the surface, fragments of my thoughts from the morning.

"Show me the dream where I was attacked," I whispered, half-fearing what would happen.

The surface of the bowl went dark, and then, like a dimmer switch was being slowly turned, the inside of an office appeared. It was the hotel manager's office, and Jimmy Leak looked up to see me standing there.

"What do you want?" he asked.

"You need to stop the 'Con. Now." I put the weight of my princess authority behind it, but he only laughed. Then his laughter turned mocking and triumphant, and I backed away.

His eyes went yellow, and he said in the cadence I'd come to recognize as belonging to my foe, "You think that will stop me, Princess? I'm having too much fun. These human minds are delicious, especially at the height of their creativity and drama."

"You need to leave them alone. This is between you and me."

In a blink, he moved from behind the desk and had his hand around my neck. The observer-me felt the power drain from the dream-me at his contact, and I shuddered.

"Tonight. At the ball. You and me, Princess. We'll have our song and dance, and then you'll come to me willingly. Otherwise I will destroy your friends."

I tried to come out of the vision, and with horror, recognized I spoke to the creature in real time, and it held me there.

My hands clawed at the invisible grip around my throat. "Let me go."

More nasty laughter. "Never. And here's a final present for you."

I found myself able to breathe again, but now I stood outside the cottage I'd seen the last time and had a wider view. Rhys pulled the hood over his head and signaled to two Fae, who were waiting in the forest nearby.

Oh, no no nonono... I tried to grab him, but my hands passed right through his wrist. He banged on the door, and a man who looked like an older version of Lawrence opened it.

"Go away. I told you, I'm not the one you're searching for."

"You look like him and talk like him, mate. And now you'll pay for what you did to me. What you did to my face."

I tried to push Rhys away from the door, but my hands met smooth stone. Cold water sloshed over my arms and onto my lap and brought me back into the present.

15

REINE

S ir Raleigh, who had been on my lap, let out an angry, "Mrrrowl!" and jumped to the floor, where he shook water from his fur. He glared at me like, *How dare you do this to me again?"*

"Are you all right?" Lawrence asked me. Concern creased his brow, and I forced a smile.

"Fine. It was the soul-eater. He found a way to break into my dreams." I rubbed my eyes and mentally held the other knowledge I'd just received away from me like a stinking piece of garbage.

"What did he say?" Kestrel asked. Since I'd touched her with my magic earlier, I could feel the fear and helplessness coming off of her. She hated that she couldn't control her powers, that she couldn't settle on just one and help. It might have saved her mother if she had been better able to manage...

I pulled out of her mental energy stream. She'd sucked me in fast with another type of power surge. Had it been mesmerizing power, or that of strong illusion and emotional capture driven by strong feeling?

Poor kid. I wished I could help her, train her, but there was no time, at least not as much as we needed.

"He said he'd see me at tonight's ball, and I'd go with him willingly. If I didn't, he'd destroy my friends."

"Don't go," Rhys growled. We all turned and glared at him. "What? You can't risk yourself for them, Reine."

"I most certainly can, and we'll figure out how to defeat him. We just need a plan."

I finally had the courage to look directly at Lawrence, and pain split the center of my chest. I finally had the answer he so desperately wanted, of what happened to his father and why, but if I told him, he'd make me choose between him and Rhys. No, he'd never do something so manipulative, especially since he valued family so highly. He'd quietly step out of my life, and the thought made me want to simultaneously cry and vomit. For the first time, I recognized the small glimmer of hope that I could have it all—a return to Faerie and the opportunity to continue exploring the spark between us. I knew there had to be a solution. I was a Fae princess.

A Fae princess being targeted by a nasty creature who had too much power due its release by dark and not only light, but High Light, Fae.

I sighed. "I think we're out of options. I need to bring in the vampires."

"Vampires?" both Kestrel and Aria squeaked.

"They're real?" Kestrel asked.

"Yes, but they're not sexy like the movies make them out to be," I lied. The last thing I needed was for her to seek out vampires for her pain.

"Don't do it, Reine." Lawrence's voice came to me like a caress. "It's not worth giving that creature your blood."

"We'll have an unbreakable contract," I said. "Limited quantity, one bite only." I rubbed my neck, dreading the experience.

Not to mention if anyone in Faerie found out about it, I could be shunned.

"That's disgusting." Rhys wrinkled his nose. "You'd actually consider bringing those filthy creatures into this?"

"Those filthy creatures, as you're calling them, are not susceptible to the soul-eater's influence because they're already dead."

"Interesting," Aria murmured. "How can I help?"

"You and Kestrel and Lady Sparkle can stay as far away from the ball tonight as you can," I said. "It's too dangerous. The soul-eater will use your connection with me against all of us."

She and Kestrel crossed their arms and set their jaws in twin expressions of rebellion.

"There's no way you're doing that, is there?" I asked.

"Nope," Aria said with a grin. "I have some ideas. Can Kestrel stay here for the day, help me make some plans and spells?"

"I have no problem with that. I'm not her parent."

"But I'm her uncle," Lawrence put in. "Well, adopted uncle. And I still say it's too dangerous, so no."

Kestrel turned her charm on. "What if we make things that y'all can use but that we don't need to be there for?"

Lawrence sighed. "I suppose that will be all right."

"Good," I said and stood. "If you don't mind, Lawrence, I'm going to catch a ride back with Rhys. I have some things to talk to him about."

Lawrence walked over to my side of the table and pecked me on the cheek. "And I have some things I want to discuss with you this afternoon. Like this crazy idea of bringing in vampires."

"Fine," I said, although I didn't plan to back down. My cheek tingled where he'd kissed me. "See you at the hotel."

Rhys waited until we'd gotten into his car and drove away. With a wave of his hand, he caused the breeze from the convertible's movement to form a shield around us. It still cooled but kept anyone from hearing our conversation. Meanwhile, I told Sir Raleigh to hide in case someone saw him from the outside and reported us for not having him in a carrier. With a huff, he jumped down to the floorboards and curled up behind my feet.

"What did you see?" Rhys asked. "Other than the soul-eater. There was something else." He scowled. "I could feel it had something to do with me, like yesterday."

I opened my mouth, my words caught in between the desire to know the truth and the fear of its ramifications. Finally, I dislodged them. "I saw you and two other Fae go to a cottage where a gargoyle lived with his family. I know what you did to him...to Lawrence's father."

I held my breath, waiting for his reaction. Would it be denial? I wanted him to deny his actions so I could still have some doubt. Or tell me it had been a different cottage, not the one belonging to Lawrence and his family. Not that I wanted another gargoyle family to have suffered like Lawrence's, but at least there wouldn't be a big, horrible secret between us.

"Right, I thought your friend looked familiar. So, I killed a gargoyle." Rhys shrugged. "Not that it mattered. I'm still scarred and in exile."

My jaw dropped for a second before I sputtered, "How could you be so cavalier about it?"

"I'm not cavalier—I'm only stating the facts, which you need to remind yourself of. Fae and gargoyles don't mix. Bad stuff happens when they do."

"Do you even know if that's who scarred you?" I asked.

"It wasn't," Rhys murmured, so softly I wouldn't have heard him if not for Fae hearing. "If it had been, I would have found peace."

I sat back and crossed my arms. "And when did you figure out that little gem?"

"Soon after I'd done it. I got a message brought to me by a courier that said, 'Nice try, but you still didn't get the designer of your visage.' But even before that, I knew. His blood, when I spilled it, didn't have the right song."

I rubbed my eyes, behind which a headache started to form. "You killed an innocent creature and sent his family into hiding for nothing."

"They deserved it. Even if it wasn't him, they must have been related. Gargoyle families have strong resemblances to each other. That's why I don't trust your paramour."

I turned to him. From this angle, with the way American cars had the driver's seat positioned, his profile appeared perfect with no scar. Aside from the hardness at the corner of his mouth from too much frowning and negative life experience, he could have been the beautiful Fae prince he'd once been. I'd spent centuries resenting him for his carelessness, which had resulted in my exile, but I hadn't given much thought to his feelings beyond his anger and desire for revenge. Now I could see the longing we shared for Faerie. For home.

"So that gargoyle you killed. Was there a little boy there? Rhys, I need to know."

"Yes. Yes, Reine. I killed Lawrence's father in front of his son."

"Ugh." Now the ugly truth would hang like a dark curtain between us. What was I supposed to do with it?

"You can't tell him." Rhys slowed to a stop at a red light and turned to me. Now I saw both sides of his face—beautiful and scarred.

"Why not?" I challenged, wanting to make him squirm now. "You know how these things go. It's going to come out eventually. Fate has been showing it to me for a reason."

"Fate's a bitch."

"Don't I know it? But seriously, why not?"

He shook his head. "Because although I don't trust him, and I don't like him, and I definitely don't think he's good enough for you, I see how he looks at you. And worse, I see how you look back."

Panic rose from my gut. "No. No, you're seeing things. You've been watching too many human romantic comedies." We couldn't have become that attached, could we?

"It's a Fae-worthy conundrum, sis." The light changed, and he returned to facing forward. "I don't want you to be hurt more than you have been, but I don't see how that's possible."

Of course, he stopped short of admitting that it was his fault that we were in this mess to begin with, stuck in this realm with little choice about interacting with its creatures, human and otherwise. I'd tried the lone Fae thing for a while, gone deep into the forest back in the nineteenth century when humans discovered industrialization and began to pollute nature in a big way. Finally, loneliness had driven me out, and I'd returned to the forest around Lycan Village.

"I need to drive him away." I pressed the heels of my hands to my eyes like that would stop the tears. "I'm going to have to be a bitch and make sure he doesn't fall in love with me."

"Probably too late for that," my oh-so-helpful little brother said.

"Then I need to make sure he doesn't become even more attached to me. Plus, I don't want him around the final confrontation with the soul-eater."

"You can be a Fae with me. You don't have to pretend you're trying to protect him if you want him gone for your own sake."

I wasn't pretending, but I didn't feel like explaining. "Hop on the interstate here. Maybe we can beat them back."

16

LAWRENCE

I watched Reine and Rhys leave through the store and listened as the crystals sang to them. My attachment to the element of earth gave me interesting little glimpses like that sometimes. The crystals also talked to me. While I couldn't quite make out what they were trying to say—I was too out of practice with using the gargoyle part of my brain—I smiled at the tone and cadence, like they tried to share juicy tidbits of gossip with me. The large black onyx bowl, however, remained silent no matter how hard I looked at it or tried to nudge it with my mind.

"You have a strong earth connection," Aria said. "Would you like to try a scrying?"

"Ah, thank you, but no." I backed away. "My talents do not lie in that direction."

"Oh, come on, Uncle Lawrence," Kestrel teased. Her impish smile and the sparkle in her blue eyes reminded me of her mother. I'd learned to say no to Bev, but Kestrel had had a piece of my heart wrapped around her little finger since she was a baby, and now I'd do anything if it would distract her from her grief. How had it been two days since the murder in the lab? It simultaneously felt like a lifetime and a blink of Earth's eye.

"Very well, I'll try." I sat on the chair Reine had vacated and found it to still be warm. Her scent eddied in the air around me, of rain and spring breezes that carry a hint of whatever's blooming nearby. "Now what?"

Aria gently placed my hands on either side of the bowl. The smooth stone quickly warmed under my touch so that it felt like a living thing. The medium then poured water into it from her crystal picture, bringing the level back to where it had been before Reine had spilled it. I could feel the heft of the bowl. What had she seen that had disturbed her to the point of knocking the heavy piece off-balance?

I hadn't meant for the question to transfer to the bowl, but it did. I saw my parents' old cottage and shadowy figures moving around it. No faces, only cloaked figures, although I strained to make out anything that would give me clues to my father's murderers and their leader.

"What does this have to do with Reine?" I asked in my mind.

The scene went dark, and I heard Ted's voice as though he stood next to me—*If you continue on your current course with the Fae, you'll have the answer to an old puzzle, but you'll also be hurt more deeply than you can imagine.*

Reine knew something about my father's murder. Anger and relief warred within me. How could she know and not tell me? Or what if she'd only found out in her vision? But then why would she go off with Rhys rather than giving me the answer to the question that had been haunting me for centuries?

My mind skirted around the possibility that Rhys had been one of the Fae. What cause would he have? Unless he thought my father had had something to do with his maiming, the gargoyle who'd helped the fake Templar scar him. But my father hadn't been at Culloden, had he? As far as I knew, the elementals had stayed out of the conflict, leaving the lycan-thropes and wizards to destroy themselves and each other.

I wished I could reach my mother and my other family, but they were in the Aerie, a hidden place that might or might not be in another dimension. Even if it was on Earth, it might as well be in another dimension considering they didn't have internet or cell signals. The only way to reach it was to hike twenty miles into a national park in a remote section of the Appalachian Mountains and then fly.

With a sound like a thunderclap, I returned to the room at the back of Aria's crystal shop and opened my eyes, which I hadn't realized were closed. Aria and Kestrel sat on my right and left, and they both studied my face with wide, eager expressions.

"Did you see anything interesting, Uncle Lawrence?" Kestrel asked.

"I... I'll need time to sort it out."

Kestrel liked Reine, and the Fae had promised to help her, had indeed already started training her. How could I take that away?

"Here," Aria said and passed a plate of oatmeal raisin cookies to me. "I could feel the magic in your vision. You need to ground yourself back in the physical world by eating something."

"You didn't give Reine cookies," Kestrel pointed out.

"She's a Fae. She doesn't need them. She's permanently between two worlds and can ground herself in either when she wishes without our help."

"Thank you." I helped myself to a cookie. As I chewed, the slight dizziness I hadn't even noticed until Aria mentioned the need for grounding dissipated.

"You're welcome. All right, Kestrel, what kind of charms and spells should we make?"

The two of them left me alone with my thoughts and the

cookies, and I took another one. It didn't help to calm the swirl of questions in my brain. By the time I finished, I decided I needed to have more than one serious conversation with Reine. First, figure out a plan without involving the vampires. Second, find out what she knew about my father's murder. Third—this was for me—stick with the previous order of things, no matter how badly I wanted to switch it around.

Would I be strong enough to do so? I supposed I would find out.

SINCE ARIA'S shop was near a MARTA line, I took the train back up to the Perimeter area so I'd have time to think through my options and strategies. However, once it emerged from the underground part of the red line, my cell phone dinged with a text from John—*"Call me. Urgent."*

Making a phone call would be breaking the rules, although people did it all the time. In spite of it being a Saturday, the train was mostly empty with only one African American guy on the opposite end of the car. He bopped his head along to whatever came through his earbuds, and I wasn't even sure he'd noticed me through his half-lidded eyes. I stuck my earbuds in and called John.

"What's up?" I asked.

"Where are you?" was his response.

"On MARTA around Lindbergh, why?"

"Can you hop off there?" John asked just as the train slowed. "I have a favor to ask you."

"Sure," I said without thinking, so I added, "Although I do have things to do and stuff to catch you up on. What do you need?"

"Lucius has been released and wants to talk to me. I need

you there so I don't throat-punch him. I'll pick you up at Lindbergh since he lives nearby."

"Right, I'll meet you at the corner of Piedmont and Sidney Marcus."

He must have already been on the way because I only waited for a few minutes.

"Why were you on the train?" he asked as I got into the car, a navy-blue BMW.

"Long story. Got stranded." Reine hadn't even thought about how I'd get back to the hotel. That hurt, although it obviously wasn't a problem.

"That sounds like a story." He rubbed the two days' worth of scruff on his angular face. His beard sparkled with gray, a reminder of how my lifespan was many times that of my human friends, even when their existence wasn't cut short by a madman with a gun.

Speaking of madmen... "I'll tell you after. What does Lucius want?"

John snorted. "He says he can explain and maybe help. What could he possibly explain? He killed my wife and wants to justify himself before he goes to court."

I didn't want to bring him back to the awful moment, but I reminded him, "She was about to say something about having help when he shot her."

"I don't know what she was talking about. Who would have helped her with such an awful project?"

I didn't want to respond, although the answer popped into my head and demanded to be expressed. "Plenty of scientists who are looking for a leg up or funds from a not-too-scrupulous industry connection. You know how competitive our field is, as secret as it is. There would be a market for what the Shadow Project would have eventually developed."

"That wasn't Beverly, though. She wanted to help our daughter."

"And you know she went to extreme lengths for it. Listen, John, if you're going to have a useful conversation with Lucius, you need to have a clear head about it."

"Be a scientist, not a man, huh?"

"You could say that."

"Like Lucius did."

John's words brought me back to my orientation at the CPDC. It had just been me, him, and Beverly, all two plus decades younger. Lucius, the new head of the unit, had handed around the stacks of notes from the slide presentation, which had been on transparency sheets at that point. As I recalled, he'd been so young and earnest at the time.

"Right," he'd said, "I get it—we all have our challenges that come from who we are, what we are. But here we're all scientists working toward the same goal, a better world through knowledge. I don't have time to go through all of this with you, so I trust you to study the materials and then ace the quiz, which will be open book, but timed."

John and Beverly had nodded, and their hands had found each other's under the desk. They'd been newlyweds at that point. I'd ignored them, feeling like they wouldn't want a not-so-young gargoyle hanging around them, but after that, we'd reviewed the policy materials and helped each other prepare. We'd also later found that the CPDC was the only branch of the CDC that required testing after orientation and worked together to change that. Nothing built bonds like going up against a seemingly impossible task.

And that brought me back to Reine. What did she know? Would she tell me? Instinct said she would be more inclined to protect her brother. My inner gargoyle had been strangely quiet that day, like the presence of the mysterious Fae had made him/me not want to poke out and tempt fate. More disturbingly, whereas the previous day he'd wanted me to fly back to the hotel and claim Reine as my mate, now he wanted me to wait and see what would happen. If I thought too hard about it, I got dizzy. I wasn't accustomed to that side of me acting according to logic and caution.

John pulled into Lucius Cimex's driveway, where a policeman lounged against his car.

"Is there a problem, Officer?" John asked.

"You the dead woman's husband?" the policeman asked.

Both John and I flinched before he replied, "Yes, that's me."

"Go on in." The cop returned his attention to his cell phone and mumbled, "We've been expecting you."

"I thought you said he was out on bond," I said.

"Guess not. Since when does anything work normally with our group?"

"True, but not like this." Our little cadre of scientists had seemed insulated from the goings on of the outside world, aside from the funding scramble that everyone had to deal with. What had happened?

Lucius opened the door. His hair was wet, and he wore an untucked button-down shirt and jeans. When he turned to us, light flashed across the round lenses of his glasses, and I shivered, remembering Reine's description of the light in Sparkle's eyes when the soul-eater had possessed her.

Lucius and John stood and regarded at each other for a long moment. Both men appeared weighed down by their respective sorrow. Even so, tension thrummed in the air between them. Not that it was entirely new. As time had progressed and Lucius had gotten more caught up in the political side of his position, there had been more conflict, more arguments over how money would be spent and other resources allocated. They'd almost come to blows once over a certain project John had wanted to do but Lucius didn't think was worthy of an internal grant.

Lucius spoke first, his normally tenor voice deepened by exhaustion. "Thank you for coming. I need to give you some context for what happened the other night. Please, come in."

He stepped aside. How could he speak so calmly, be so detached? I'd always known he had a spirit of steel beneath his nice guy exterior, but could he have been a sociopath all along without anyone knowing?

No, the witches, who could read auras, would have been able to tell something was off. Or maybe they'd never peeked at his out of respect for his privacy.

"Can I get you anything?" he asked when we were inside and seated in his living room. Again, the incongruity of the situation struck me. He'd hosted parties twice a year, once at the holidays and a summer barbecue. He'd never answered the door without wearing an apron and a broad smile, and before anyone knew it, he'd pressed cocktails into our hands—iced tea when Beverly was pregnant—and brought us out to his sun room or back porch. Then I'd help him bring trays of food out from the kitchen because there had never been a Mrs. Cimex, and we bachelors have to stick together, right? Lucius and I had never talked about why we were single, but I'd often wondered. He'd always seemed nice enough, at least in social situations. I added another tick to the "hidden dark side" column.

John and I declined beverages and sat on the navy-blue couch in the living room, which had a nautical theme. Lucius took the dark brown leather recliner. John perched on the edge of the cushion, his fists clenched on his knees, and glared at Lucius, who placed one ankle over the other knee and leaned back, his fingers steepled. I had the odd sense that while we'd come to talk to and challenge him, he had control over the situation. But he'd been in the wrong, hadn't he? Gargoyles found drama both fascinating and repulsive—another reason it hadn't worked out between us and the Fae—so I couldn't have left if I tried.

Lucius spoke first, his southern drawl conveying utmost sorrow. "John, first let me say how truly sorry I am."

"Sorry?" John didn't raise his voice, but his tone held all the tension of screaming. "You shot and killed Beverly, and all you can say is *sorry*?"

"I told you I had answers, and I'll get to them, but first I wanted to apologize. While my actions were not entirely my own on Thursday evening, I had long ago opened the door for something to influence me."

"What do you mean?" I asked. John trembled, and I placed a gentle hand on his forearm to steady him. He nodded thanks, but shoved my hand away, never taking his gaze from our former boss.

Lucius looked down, and when his eyes met mine and then John's, they shimmered with tears. "I'd long ago become attracted to Beverly." He waved a hand, presumably gesturing to his empty house. "I've never had a wife. No time to date with the job, you see. And so, she was the major female influence in my life, and I became attached."

"Gods." John rubbed his hands over his face. "Did she... Did you and she...?"

I couldn't move. Had Beverly reciprocated Lucius' feelings? Could I have been so enthralled in my own work I missed something I should have seen? Memory after memory of interactions between Lucius and Beverly flashed through my brain, but nothing had ever seemed amiss.

"No," Lucius said. "I never told her of my feelings for her. We were too good a team to ruin it with the drama of an affair or the discomfort it would create if I were to express my desires, and she had spurned them."

"So you killed her?" John's incredulity cracked the last syllable. "I'd say you pretty well fucking ruined the team, Lucius."

Lucius dropped his foot to the floor and leaned forward, elbows on knees and hands folded across his forehead. "That had never been my intention. I could never willingly hurt Beverly." He tilted his head up, anguish in his expression. "And I could never say no to her, either. That's why when she asked for my help with Kestrel, I gave her access to all the laboratory resources and covered up after the Chronic Lycanthropy Syndrome had been made to disappear into the hands of industry."

"That means you knew about the Shadow Project all along," I said. "Why did you allow the vector to get out?"

"Beverly needed money for the research, and I had fudged the numbers as much as I could. If you'll recall, that was about the time the administration changed, and we suddenly faced massive budget cuts. The money from Cabal allowed not just the Shadow Project, but all our projects to keep going until we could figure out the funding situation."

John shook his head. "And you killed her to keep all this from coming out?"

"No!" Lucius' denial echoed through the room. "I didn't intend to kill her. I didn't even intend to shoot her. Something came over me. Something with its own agenda to sew chaos and pain..." He buried his head in his hands, and his shoulders shook with sobs, through which three words emerged: "I've ruined everything."

I glanced at John, who seemed more shocked than angry. "Do you believe him?" he mouthed.

"I'm afraid I do. He did seem to be possessed, then disoriented." Hmmm, where had I seen that before? Once it had attacked me and killed the security guard, it should have weakened. It should have returned to wherever it went to recharge, but what if it had stayed around, had somehow gotten past the wards around the lab? Or had never left?

Lucius' crying subsided, and he slowly straightened and wiped his smeared glasses with his shirttail. Then he stood. "I'll be right back."

John and I looked at each other again, and John scowled. I had some idea of what he could be feeling. Everyone wanted answers to their tragedies. He was lucky—he wouldn't have to wait centuries for his.

I couldn't help it—I checked my watch. Reine should be back at the hotel by now. As much as I wanted to be there for John, I *needed* to know what she was keeping from me.

Lucius returned carrying a manila folder. "The lab alerted me that you had the wine we were drinking sent for analysis so I could authorize the charge. The results came in this afternoon. I asked them to allow me to share them with you."

17

———

REINE

Rhys and I dropped his car off with the valets and walked inside the hotel. Sir Raleigh disappeared from my shoulder, and I hoped he'd gone up to the room. I thought there had been a lot of people there yesterday, but that seemed to have been a rehearsal. Today we had to weave around clusters of 'Con-goers, all dressed up like fairies with wings and pointed ear additions. Both the men and women sported glitter on their faces and makeup highlighting cheekbones and jawlines, making their faces appear thin and angular. Rhys and I exchanged an amused glance at what they thought our world must be like.

"Damn, I left my glitter and wings in my other jacket," Rhys joked, then turned serious. "I've almost forgotten what they feel like."

I flexed my shoulder blades, remembering the feel of the lift of flight and the strength it took, even with a magical boost. "Me, too. If I tried now, I'd be too out of shape, I fear."

Rhys snorted. "That's a very human thing to say. You'd be able to fly. You're a princess—you're stronger than most."

"I wish I felt it." The revelations of the morning had

knocked the wind out of my proverbial wings and the oomph out of my Fae princess authority. Then, when he rolled his eyes, I added, "Don't make me go all Fae on your skinny ass."

"My ass isn't skinny. It's tight."

A young woman's voice nearby kept me from making another snarky reply. "Hey! You two." We turned to see a troop of forest elves with brown leather vests and corsets over green puffy-sleeved shirts. They also wore soft brown pants and boots, and each had a wreath of fake greenery around his or her head and fake ear tips.

Rhys didn't try to hide his laugh. "Great, it's the Fae scouts."

"Or the gnome-keteers," I murmured, then elbowed him. "Be nice. We may need their help."

They surrounded us, and the leader folded his arms and looked us up and down. I frowned—his beady brown eyes reminded me of someone, but I couldn't recall who.

"What do you think you're supposed to be?" he asked

"Uh, Fae," Rhys said. "Isn't it obvious?"

"In human clothes? The queen would be so disappointed."

Someone shoved me aside, and I almost sent a reflexive kneeling spell their way, but then saw Lady Sparkle. Correction —a pissed off Lady Sparkle.

"Lay off of them, Kyle," she said. "You have no idea what you're doing."

Kyle's face turned red. "Don't call me that, Katie. I mean Lady Sparkle. And I'm only enforcing the Fairy code, that all here must present as they are and not try to hide behind human trappings."

"This isn't your 'Con, Corvid. You don't make the rules."

"That's Prince Corvid to you."

Rhys nearly doubled over laughing. "You? A Fae prince? Oh, I'm sorry, 'fairy prince.'" He exaggerated the air quotes. "Why don't you go find some singing animals to kiss and see if they turn into pretty girls for you?"

While part of me was grateful he'd limited his suggestion to kissing the animals—anything more would have gotten him kicked out—I didn't want to draw attention to ourselves by prolonging the interaction. However, the groups near us had grown silent, and I felt the weight of a hundred curious human gazes. And—with the feeling of cold fingers across the back of my neck—that of the soul-eater, who relished the challenge. Perhaps it had even sneaked into Kyle/Corvid's psyche and planted the idea.

I grabbed Rhys' hand and sent him a bolt of secret conversation— *"Careful, it's here."*

"Noted."

The sensation of a wall going down around and between us reminded me to try to lock down my own psyche so the soul-eater couldn't try to influence me. That had been one advantage of its earlier invasion of my vision—I'd at least found one psychic door it could use and knew how to close it. I was sure it wouldn't waste its strength in the current interaction, but I also knew blocking it could provoke it. Indeed, Corvid's eyes flashed yellow, and his lips pulled into a non-human snarl.

"What are you saying, *peasant*?" Corvid growled.

Lady Sparkle glanced up at me, her expression concerned. "Is it here?" she whispered. I nodded.

"Nothing." Rhys put his hands in his pockets and smiled, although not nicely. "But I'd suggest you take Silly, Dopey, and Sneezy and toddle along before you get in real trouble here."

I wanted so badly to kick him in the shin. He just couldn't resist the opportunity to provoke someone and prove how clever he was. On one level, I understood—it was how he expressed the pent-up anger and resentment at his exile. But this wasn't helping my strategy of lying low.

Rhys snapped his fingers, and Corvid toppled like someone had punched the backs of both his knees. Now the angry glare came from both Corvid and the soul-eater. "You'll regret that."

"Don't mess with a true Fae prince," Rhys said, then turned to leave and bumped into Samir.

"What's going on here?" Samir asked.

Dazed, Corvid stumbled to his feet. The monster had left, leaving the bully behind. "He hit me," Corvid slurred.

"He didn't touch him," Lady Sparkle said. "We all saw it."

Samir didn't allow the argument to continue in public. "All of you, in my office. Now."

IN A FEW MINUTES, the five of us—Corvid, Sparkle, Rhys, Samir, and I—stood in a curtained-off area behind the main registration table. The noises of the 'Con—people laughing, talking, debating—swirled around us, but muffled. I knew our enemy also prowled through the place, searching for opportunities to sneak in and feed off negative energy. Even our brief interaction had left me feeling shaky, but then, it had been a rough morning, and I needed food. If such a short encounter had weakened me, how was I supposed to manage a battle at a ball?

Well, first thing—make sure the ball wouldn't happen. Samir's aristocratic black brows, drawn together with exhaustion and annoyance, told me it wouldn't be easy to convince him.

"What happened?" Samir asked, but not to anyone in particular. Both Sparkle and Corvid jumped in, and Samir held up a hand. "Corvid, why don't you start?"

"We were having a conversation, and he didn't like what I was saying, so he hit me."

"Where did he hit you?"

"Well, it was more of a kick. In the back of the knees."

Samir arched an eyebrow. "While he stood in front of you?"

Corvid spoke through clenched teeth. "He's fast."

Samir sighed. "Lady Sparkle?"

She crossed her arms. "Corvid's pulling his same crap as usual—giving people with what he considers the 'wrong costume' a hard time."

"It's all in good fun," Corvid argued. "I'm just trying to help."

"Corvid, we've talked about this. Not at my 'Con. Now get out of my sight. Even better, why don't you leave for the rest of the day?"

Corvid's face went beyond red to purple. "But, but..."

"No buts. And if I see you again today or hear of one more incident, you're banned for life. Got it?" Samir stood and held a curtain aside. "Now get out."

"This wasn't due process! I'm going to register a complaint." Corvid stalked through the open curtain, then turned back to Samir. I wanted him to make a threat and get banned, but he only shook his head and left. Samir allowed the curtain to fall and turned toward me, Rhys, and Sparkle.

"Let me guess, more role-playing?" he asked.

I dialed up my Fae charm. "Thank you for taking care of that," I said. "He just confronted us with no provocation."

Samir glowered at us. "I've wanted to ban him for a while, and I thought I'd get my chance this year, but he's the hotel manager's nephew. Whatever you did, right or wrong, to attract his attention, you've made a mess for me."

"Are you seriously victim-blaming us?" Lady Sparkle practically quivered with anger. "They didn't do anything."

"It's true," Rhys said. "We'd only just walked in when they surrounded us."

"And what happened, he fell?" Samir gave us one of his skeptical looks. He was good at that.

Rhys couldn't completely hide his smug smile. "Appears as though he tripped over something."

"While standing still." Samir pinched the bridge of his nose. "I don't know what you two are up to, but you need to dial it back. Especially you, Rhys. I've had complaints."

Rhys shrugged and said with a thick accent, "I apologize. Where I come from, we have different concepts of personal space."

Samir rubbed his temples, and I nudged Rhys to dial back the glamour.

"He'll be more careful," I promised. "I do have a request."

With a sigh, Samir said, "I'm sure you do. We're not canceling the rest of the 'Con."

"No, that's fine. I just need you to call off tonight's party."

Samir looked at us for a long moment, then shook his head. "Sorry, kids, can't do that."

"Please." I held up a hand. "It's going to be a disaster if it goes on. There could be a big battle, and I don't want anyone to be hurt."

"A big battle." Samir shook his head. "Whatever your game is, I don't have time to be a part of it."

"Can you at least show us the precautions you're taking to keep everyone safe?" Lady Sparkle asked.

"Remember, we have permission from the hotel manager to see behind-the-scenes," I added, then appended mentally, *for now*. Had the soul-eater known that Corvid was Jimmy Leak's nephew and chosen him to cause trouble? It wouldn't surprise me.

"Fine." Samir gestured for us to follow him, which we did. He nodded and greeted people along the way, and I watched for yellow flashes in eyes and snarls moving across faces but didn't see any. Samir brought us to a meeting room and unlocked the door. We walked into a jumble of flowers and pieces of scenery—arches of ivy, fake tree trunks, and other faux natural things.

"Smurfy," Rhys said, resting his hand on an oversized mushroom.

Samir ignored him. "This is the prep room for the ball

tonight. Only I and my assistants have access to it for security reasons. I hate to say it, but we've had threats before."

I pondered the different ways a party could be disrupted and attendees harmed. "And what about food and drinks and whatnot?"

He brought us to a door in the back of the room, which he also unlocked. He led us into a space that obviously was not meant for regular hotel guests to see, as the floor went from carpet to concrete, and harsh overhead lights illuminated bare, unpainted walls. A folding table held a large punch bowl, two large plastic serving ladles, and sleeves of disposable cups. Another one was piled with serving platters and three empty chafing dishes.

"Only hotel staff has access to this room."

"And you," I pointed out.

"And me," he agreed. "And my wife, who's in charge of this part of the party. But as you can see, access is very limited. We do take security and the safety of our 'Con guests seriously."

He gave Rhys a pointed glance. Rhys put his hands in his pockets and shrugged. Fae didn't normally get headaches, but he was going to give me one if he kept up. But he also couldn't help who and what he was. My mother had spoiled him, and I... well, I'd probably gone too easy on him since his injury since I felt badly for him. Together, we'd created this spoiled Fae monster who, I had to admit, still had his good moments.

We followed Samir out through the decorations room and back into the hallway off the main space. We hung out in the shadows and watched the flow of people beyond. Some appeared happy, some pensive, some determined... It struck me how they would be sad to go back to their regular lives after FaeCon was over, mourning their return to the very situation I craved.

"Is there anything else you need?" Samir asked.

"Besides for you to cancel the ball?" I gave him a hopeful smile.

"Out of the question. Hopefully you feel a little better now that I've shown you that we keep everything secure until it's time."

"Would it be possible for me to have access to those rooms this evening?"

"I suppose, if you still have the hotel manager's permission." He shook his head as he left and muttered, "Of all the people..."

"Thanks." Hopefully I could draw the soul-eater away from the party and into the back room, where we could tangle one-on-one. And with a vampire's help.

That reminded me—I needed to get in touch with Ashlee Wyatt, or at least her daytime assistant.

The thought of her fangs anywhere near my neck made me shiver, but what other choice did I have?

Rhys and I walked back toward the lobby. I watched for any sign of trouble, either from my main enemy or Corvid's gnome crew but didn't see any.

"You're pale, sis. Do you need food?"

Yep, he had his good moments. "Yes, please. But let's eat down here. I want to keep an eye on things."

Sure, we'd have lunch, and then I'd contact Ashlee's people. No, I wasn't putting off reaching out to her—well, to our liaison Ted Steele—at all.

18

LAWRENCE

Lucius opened the folder and raised his eyebrows as he studied the results.

"Come on," John snapped, "we all know you've already looked at them."

"I wanted to make sure I understand them correctly." Lucius closed the file and handed it to John, who snatched it from him and opened it.

I read along with him. "Neoline, mesaconitine..." I blinked, and the significance of the compounds hit me. "These are alkaloids of aconite."

"Right, gentlemen." Lucius had returned to scientist-lecturer mode. "Wolfsbane, which legendarily has been used to promote out-of-body experiences."

"And is toxic," John added.

"But not in small doses," I said. "And these amounts are minimal. I've heard about some shifters using it to astral project their animal sides instead of physically changing." I couldn't imagine doing so. It seemed an invitation to get stuck permanently, at least for us gargoyles. I always needed my entire *awake* mental faculties to resist the urge to stay shifted.

"Yes," Lucius agreed. "And think about what could happen if it were combined with the impulse control inhibition of alcohol. Rather than sending spirits out, it could open the door to allow something in."

"You're saying you shot Beverly because you were possessed." John closed the folder. "I'm supposed to believe that?" But he didn't sound as sternly doubtful as he had previously.

"We're currently dealing with a creature who could do that," I told him. "What if it had an accomplice in the lab who laced the wine so it could? Then it could attack, make us think it was too weak to strike again, and use the aconite to make it easier to sneak into your psyches."

"You weren't drinking, John," Lucius pointed out.

John's jaw dropped. "You can't be accusing me. I had no idea of any of this. Why would I have pursued the toxicology results if I'd done it? I'd just be incriminating myself."

Lucius leaned forward. "You've been sleep-deprived. That, too, can lower inhibitions and possibly allow an opening for something to creep in. Can you account for your whereabouts and every conscious moment on Thursday?"

"I... I think so." But he'd gone pale. "I don't know. I walked outside to get some air that afternoon, and it seemed that I blinked and was back in my office. I thought it was a trick of my mind—I'd been lost in deep thoughts about my current project, and I've done that before, gone on autopilot—but now I'm not sure."

"That would explain how you knew to search for something in the wine," I said. "Your subconscious told you."

John dropped his face into his hands, his elbows on his knees. "But then that means that *I'm* the one who killed Beverly."

"No!" Lucius stood. "It was that creature Lawrence and Doctor River are hunting, not you. This was part of its plan to sew chaos and separation. This is when it's important to pull together, not get lost in self-recrimination and accusations."

John raised his head and narrowed his eyes. "That's easy for you to say, Lucius. You're the one who's going to go to jail for pulling the trigger."

"And you're the one who may accompany me for lacing the wine."

"No," I said. "You have no proof. The evidence is all circumstantial, and everyone's fingerprints were on the bottle."

"Plus, I don't remember doing it," John said. "Maybe I didn't. Maybe you did, and you're trying to manipulate me into admitting to something I didn't do." He stood, and I did so as well. "Thanks for sharing the results. That was enlightening." He turned, and Lucius put a hand on his shoulder.

"Wait! Where are you going?"

"I need to get Lawrence back to the hotel so he can help the Fae capture the creature."

"But do you forgive me?"

John turned back toward him. "I don't know. No matter what influence you may have been under, you still had enough desire to hurt Beverly to allow the soul-eater to act through you. I don't know if I can ever forgive you for that."

We'd just gotten to John's car and buckled in when my phone dinged with a text from Ted.

"The Fae just asked me to set something up with Ashlee for sunset. You aware of this?"

"Hurry," I said. "We need to get back before Reine makes a big mistake."

~

When we arrived back at the hotel, I dashed up the stairs to our room because I didn't want to wait in line at the elevator. I found Reine sitting on the bed with Sir Raleigh on her lap. She started to rise, and the cat gave her a baleful look before gracefully leaping to the floor and licking his shoulder.

"Hey, I thought we were going to talk about the vampire plan before moving forward," I said. "I got a text from Ted. Oh, and the tox results came in."

She gazed at me for a long moment, then stood, her fingers hooked in the pockets of her jeans. She wore the neutral, yet slightly haughty expression I'd come to associate with the Fae, and anger sparked in my chest.

"Aren't you going to say anything? We had an agreement."

"We agreed to discuss it." She tilted her chin up, which made her next words more condescending. "Certain things have come to light, and I felt it best to move forward."

Who was this cold creature, so opposite from the flame I'd danced with the evening before? As a creature of stone and water, I should have been able to read her shifting mood and see better underneath the cool, confident exterior she projected when she wanted to hide her true intent. But that had been our dance, hadn't it? Misdirection, confusion, misinterpretation. Guessing. So much damn guessing...

"We're supposed to be working on this *together*," I reminded her, barely keeping my own tone neutral. My inner gargoyle rumbled, ready for a fight, but I kept him in check.

"I've decided to proceed on my own. I won't be needing your help."

That did it. I didn't raise my voice—I never yelled at women—but my feelings burst out of me. "Like hell you don't! What about this morning?"

"The gray Fae would have helped me. He's connected to me somehow." But I heard her doubt.

Then the vision from the bowl came back to me. "This is about what you saw while you scried at Aria's this morning, isn't it? Why won't you tell me?" The last word came out with a hint of growl.

"It's not the time."

"Oh, that's a classic Fae answer. You know something. Something that I've..." I took a deep breath. "The answer I've been seeking for centuries. Centuries, Reine. Do you know what that's like, to want something so badly for so long it takes Herculean effort to not allow it to consume every waking moment? To shoehorn a life around it but always feeling like you're on the outside because you've got this one part missing?"

She crossed her arms. "I do, Lawrence. And that's why I have to ask you to leave. Go back home." She shook her head. "Home. At least you have one. Go, I'll be in touch later."

Right, she did know how it felt. Perhaps these two missing pieces, our respective mysteries, had drawn us together in the first place. Could I wait?

Ted had mentioned a big black hole in my future, or something like that. Was I standing at its edge? Would insisting on the truth push me away, or would it tumble me head-first into trouble and pain? And what about her?

She still stood there, her arms crossed, and her face stiff with a haughty Fae expression. Except there was one thing off... A subtle twitch in her left hand and the slight motion of a lock of hair said she didn't feel as coldly as she tried to portray. I took a deep breath, opening the supernatural sense I tried to rarely use, preferring tangible scientific knowledge instead. A single fact vibrated in the air between us, that if she were to tell me what she knew, it would tear both of us apart.

My inner gargoyle growled at the thought of hurting her. Although I mentally reached for the answer to the question of who had killed my father, I drew back. Maybe I could figure out a way for the truth to come out, guide her so it wouldn't be so painful for us. Logic could win here, right? Even if what she told me devastated me, she'd likely be going to Faerie, so we'd have time to heal.

What was I thinking—likely? No, she'd return home. Fae always did.

The thought of her leaving produced a crushing sensation in my gut and propelled me to close the distance between us.

"Fine, you can tell me later, but I'm not leaving you." I caressed the edge of one of her pointed ears with a fingertip.

She closed her eyes and turned away. The sting of hurt and rejection replaced the anger.

"I can't do this, Lawrence. There's too much..." A sigh lifted and dropped her shoulders.

I gently cupped them. "There is," I agreed. "And it's not going anywhere."

She turned back to me but allowed my hands to rest again on her shoulders. "But you're not going anywhere, either, are you?"

The slight edge of hope in her words kept me from saying, *Fine, you do what you want. I can tell where I'm not wanted.* She wanted me. She *needed* me. But she didn't want to admit it.

Pain versus Answers. Hell, I was a scientist. I'd take the answers every time, and to hell with the rest. When I thought of learning the truth, I sensed a delineation of Before versus After.

Now that I was faced with this enormous turning point, I had to examine whether I was ready for everything to change. Fine, I'd put it off...but not for too long. Only until we vanquished the soul-eater. Then we could get on with the rest of our lives.

No, I could wait a few more hours to face *after*. I needed to enjoy *before* first.

I gently drew her to me, giving her every chance to back away. She didn't. She lifted her face to mine.

"Are you sure, Lawrence?"

"Yes." This time a growl of desire escaped my chest. Her green eyes blazed with need, and both my inner gargoyle and I smiled at the thought that we could make her light up like that.

"This may be our only chance," she whispered. She reached around me and untucked my shirt, then ran her hands up my back. Her fingertips blazed tingling trails across my skin. I closed my eyes, relishing the sensation, and lowered my face to hers. Our lips met, not with the hunger of the previous evening, but in gentle exploration. I wanted to move my palms from where they cupped her shoulders, but didn't want to spook her in spite of her signals that she was more than okay with what we were doing.

She withdrew from our kiss and smiled up at me. "Nervous?"

19

REINE

Gods, his muscles. How did a scientist who spent most of his time in a lab get such a defined physique? I hadn't explored his chest yet—that was next—but I could only imagine his pecs and abs. Oh, right, I had seen them, and I couldn't wait to feel them against me, nothing between us.

Except some hesitation on his part. I could feel it in his kiss, the stiffness of his hands on my shoulders.

I drew back. "Nervous?"

He swallowed, and his neck muscles showed me that they, too, had nice definition.

"I... I don't have a lot of experience," he admitted.

"Oh. I mean, it's been a while for me, but..." I grinned and traced a finger down his chest over his shirt. "Luckily you seem to have some natural talent in this direction."

He chuckled. "I'm not used to someone else being in charge, but you did well on the dance floor."

"It's okay, we can take it slowly. And don't worry, no magic like our dance. It will be all us."

He pressed his lips to mine again, and this time I was the

one who had the hesitation. If he'd been experienced and had other lovers, he would be less likely to pine away for me after I went back to Faerie, even if I returned, but if I was his first...

"Are you all right?" He trailed kisses across the oh-so-sensitive lobe of my left ear and nibbled the tip. Gods, I nearly came right there. He clasped me to him when my knees went weak, and we fell to the bed. He slid his hand up under my shirt and found my left breast. Then he lightly cupped it and ran his thumb over the tip. With his other hand, he unhooked my bra on the first try.

All right, I was definitely not his first. He continued to nibble at my ear, the right one, and gently cup and knead my breast until a wave of pleasure crashed through me, and he covered my cry with his mouth.

"You know more than you let on," I said once I could speak again. He held me against him, my back to his front, and I could feel his gargoyle-sized erection against my ass.

"I may have a little experience." He kissed the back of my neck, and desire built in me again. I turned to face him and kissed him, this time with nothing held back. With Fae quickness, I pulled his shirt off and took a moment to admire the smooth muscle.

"That's not fair," he said and tugged at the edge of my shirt. "I want to see you."

His phone dinged with a text, and he groaned, but he pulled it out of his pocket. "Fuck."

"What is it?" I asked. Pride zinged through me that I'd gotten him aroused enough to curse.

"That's Ted. He said that Rae got back to him. They want us at the club in half an hour." He looked at his watch, then at his lower abdomen, then back at me. "I need to, ah..."

"I can help you with that."

"No. If you do, I'll want to stay with you here and make love to you all night." He got up and stiffly made his way into his room and closed the door.

I lay back on the bed and took a few moments to compose myself before changing into a short, red dress. I resisted the urge to put on a turtleneck over it. When Lawrence returned, his eyes had lightened from dark with desire back to their usual gray, although his cheeks maintained their flush.

"Are you ready?" he asked.

"Yes. Well, as ready as I'm going to be."

He cupped my face, and a line of worry appeared between his brows. "You don't have to do this. We can still figure out another way."

I shook my head, which allowed me to lean into his hand. "I don't see how. We're running out of time." Both for the soul-eater and before Lawrence found out Rhys killed his father. Did he suspect? He must, and it gave me hope that he had agreed to wait for me to tell him, to tear that veil of shadows and let in the truth that would rip us apart. Could this nascent thing between us survive, after all?

Lawrence's phone dinged. He sighed and dropped his hand. "That's Ted. He's downstairs. He'll take you."

"Ted?" I stepped back, resisting the urge to cling to him. "What about you?"

"I need to get the things Kestrel and Aria prepared for us and drop Kestrel at home."

I tried to hide my disappointment that we'd be separated, but I understood. He took his responsibility as uncle seriously, another stark difference between him and the men I'd grown up around, who had been too engaged in power struggles in the court to pay much attention to their offspring. I found it sweet and terrifying.

Perhaps the result of physically connecting with him wouldn't be him pining for me. What if I was in danger of falling so hard for him, I'd never be happy in Faerie?

As expected, Ted waited for us in the drop-off zone in front of the hotel.

When I'd met Ted Steele earlier that week, he'd seemed affable, maybe a little ruthless when it came to getting the scoop on a murder. Today purple circles under his eyes and the dark brown scruff on his cheeks gave him the appearance of an exhausted criminal instead of a dapper newsman.

"You look like hell," Lawrence told him.

Ted opened the passenger side door of his red Mustang for me. "You're not much better, although you've got a certain aura about you." Ted glanced between me and Lawrence. "Guess I should've run a few minutes late, huh?"

"As if you didn't know," Lawrence grumbled. He bent to give me a kiss on the cheek through the open window. "Take good care of her. Don't let Ashlee do anything to her that she doesn't want."

Right, as if a prognosticating witch could do anything to stop a thirsty vampire. If vamp and Fae got into it, the best place for Ted would be far, far away.

Ted pulled out of the circular drive in front of the hotel, and I rolled my window up in anticipation of us going on the interstate. Instead, he took the same tree-lined route through a more residential area that Lawrence had the other night. I hadn't known what to expect, but silence wasn't it.

"Is all of Atlanta this green?" I asked. From what I'd seen, I guessed it probably was, but something about him made me want to start a conversation.

"Pretty much."

This was not the gregarious, teasing Ted of my first trip to the club. The fact he could see the future made me nervous. Did he know something, see a possible path of danger for me? For Lawrence? Whereas Southerners might be inclined to tiptoe around issues, I decided to face his sullen demeanor head-on.

"Have I done something to offend you?" Okay, that was more sideways, but at least I'd brought it up.

"No, not at all. I'm tired. Haven't been sleeping well."

"Any reason?" I sensed his evasion and attempted to put out *calm doctor* vibes, but I doubted that I succeeded. Portraying calm didn't work very well when anxiety clouded one's brain. The last time I'd encountered a prognosticating witch, I'd come to dread whenever she opened her mouth. She'd delighted in torturing me with vague predictions that could have multiple interpretations. Now, a century later, I could admit my own fault. I'd been so eager for a prediction that would tell me I was going home that I'd twisted her words into a false and ulti-mately crushing hope.

"Would you believe it's because I can't tell the future in this case?" Ted paused at a stop sign and rolled his shoulders. "When you're like me, you can usually tell big things are coming. Like I knew my brother would find happiness with someone unexpected from his past and that there would be some sort of trouble with my sister. Unfortunately, she knew how to block me—she was a locking witch and hid her own future from me."

"Was?"

He turned right on to a three-lane road. "Was. I still don't know if I could have done anything to save her, even if I'd known. That's why me not being able to see the direction of Lawrence's path bugs me so much."

Panic spiked through me. As close as Ted and Lawrence were, Ted should be able to at least sense Lawrence's future generally. "You're most worried about Lawrence. That makes me concerned, too."

"I'm glad, considering that you're the big wild card that obfuscates his future." He made a sweeping gesture with his right hand, and the car drifted into the center lane, which caused an angry honk from a fellow motorist.

I clutched the door handle. "Do you know how?"

"No." Ted corrected our course. "If I did, I'd tell you and find out how to make you stop."

As if he could. I waited for my heart rate to slow and took an inventory of what I could and should do. As for the *could*— not much. My magic was too weak here to manipulate the several-ton car if he got distracted again.

And as for *should*...

I'd delay asking more about Lawrence until after our meeting. Ted had likely already told me all he knew anyway. Hades, I should've gone with my original plan to push Lawrence away, but I couldn't do it.

20

REINE

We arrived at the club before sunset and found that there were no bouncers outside. In fact, the area felt deserted, especially for a Saturday. Strange shadows slanted around us, giving the area around the club door a cave-like air.

"Where is everyone?" I asked. Ted pulled right up to the door and cut the engine.

"Probably inside or waiting for the club to open."

I didn't wait for him to open my door for me. Instead, I got out when he did, and the sound of my door closing echoed off the concrete and brick surfaces surrounding us. It wasn't the emptiness that spooked me—it was the air of expectation along with the memories of what had happened...and what was about to. If I tried hard enough, I could still smell the blood of the bouncer the soul-eater had killed so it could spell out its threat to me in a horrific way. The queen of the hive was about to get something she'd been wanting for a long time—Fae blood—and she'd invested in some pretty hefty magic to make sure we'd be alone.

"I, ah, don't suppose you have any hints for me here, do you?" I asked, almost in a whisper.

Ted's eyes had gone unfocused, a slight crease between his brows. "Be careful. She wants you here alone. I'll have Lawrence pick you up later."

He'd been spelled, but I still tried to stop him. "Wait, what? No. Don't leave me here!"

But it was too late. He darted back into the car like a fish into a coral crease. Before I could summon my own magic to break the hold of the spell on him, he'd roared off.

"Well, Hades."

The mirrored club door opened, and Rae peeked out, wearing a light blue suit and white-framed glasses, but the lenses weren't tinted. His caution gave him the air of a schoolboy, and I wondered how old he'd been when he'd been turned. No more than mid-twenties. First he glanced sideways at the street, and I guessed he measured the angle of the sun. Even the most powerful vampire always kept an eye on his main foe—sunlight. Then when he turned his dark gaze on me, he smiled and showed his fangs. All innocence in his demeanor evaporated.

"Welcome, Princess. The mistress is expecting you." He stepped back and held the door open for me, but then frowned when he saw my purse, which contained the grimalkin. "I'll have to ask you to leave your pet outside."

"Sir Raleigh isn't my pet."

"Still, Mistress has requested no other creatures but you."

"Fine." I opened my purse, and Sir Raleigh's expression told me he didn't like the idea of leaving me alone. "Sorry, kitty, but you need to go." My purse lightened as he disappeared. As usual, I wondered where he went. Perhaps to report to whoever had sent him. I half expected to see someone else appear, but no one did.

"That's better. You may enter."

"Thank you." Although I didn't know for what. I was the one walking into a trap, after all, and now I didn't have my main defense against dark creatures.

We walked through the club, all gloom and gray. He hadn't offered to turn on any lights, and I didn't ask. We were both supernatural creatures who could see without light, after all. Could he be testing me? Whereas a human might have been thrown off, I relaxed. I couldn't remember the last time I'd been treated as what I was without having to adjust how I moved, as I'd had to mention to Rhys. Even my previous interactions with Ashlee had been partial performances for Lawrence, not wanting him to see too much of my Fae side.

As I followed Rae up the stairs, I straightened parts of my body and spirit I hadn't recognized I'd stifled and slumped, and by the time we reached the top, I finally filled out my Fae princess self. The surroundings lightened, and when I checked my hands, I found I glowed with a luminescence that shifted from blue to gold and back.

Huh. I hadn't seen that before. I didn't have time to ponder the meaning of the strange glow, however, because we emerged into Ashlee's upper room, which had been transformed from its red and black boudoir-like setting to one of cool blues and greens with plants and crystals on tables and in corners.

"Welcome, Princess," Ashlee said. "I hope you like my redecorating. I wanted you to feel comfortable about our transaction."

"It's lovely." And cold, I wanted to add, but didn't for fear of offending her. But it did feel familiar, like a place my grandmother or mother would have set up. The heavy ache of homesickness rolled through my chest, but not for Faerie. No, there was a brief longing for my little cottage outside Lycan Village and the Faerie Circle in the cave where I would meet with my mother. I hadn't properly appreciated the latter place for its unique beauty. Would I see it again before returning home?

"Excellent. May I offer you a drink?" She practically vibrated with eagerness, and I respected her etiquette.

"Yes, please. White wine."

Rae moved to the white and black marble bar against the far wall and pulled a bottle of white wine out of an ice bucket. He brought it to me and asked, "Is this all right?"

It was a bottle of white Burgundy. Did they think I'd be afraid of my drink being drugged? Should I be? I checked the label and then the foil surrounding the cork at the top. I didn't see any evidence of the foil having been tampered with, and the pressed metal didn't have any feel of being pierced or cut since being placed around the bottle.

"It looks lovely."

He made a show of removing the foil and uncorking it. Then he poured the golden liquid into a glass and handed it to me. I took a sniff with all my senses, alert for anything that shouldn't be there. Nothing out of the ordinary—only the crisp fruity scent of the wine and the sparkling sense of fermentation. The first sip cooled my tongue and warmed my stomach.

"Thank you," I said. "Before we proceed, I wanted to discuss the terms of our contract."

The only part of Ashlee that moved was one delicate eyebrow, which she arched. "I thought it was simple, Princess. I get one drink of blood from you, and we help you capture the soul-eater."

"Yes, about that." I took another sip of wine. "Is there anything else I can offer you besides my blood? I'm sure you can understand my hesitation."

Ashlee smiled. "I thought you may have reservations, so I am prepared to negotiate for more on my part."

"I don't need anything else from you."

With vampire speed, she stood in front of me, our breasts almost touching. "No, but there may be things you want," she said, her voice a seductive purr. "I sense that you have had some frustration lately with that adorable gargoyle. Rae or I would be happy to make sure you leave here satisfied in every sense."

She lifted her right hand and reached for my left ear, and her stunning ice-blue eyes warmed a shade. For a shameful moment, I considered her offer. Perhaps if I were to satisfy myself here, I could shed my attraction to Lawrence.

The impossibility of that swept through me, cold and clear. I stepped back.

"No thank you," I said, my cheeks aflame. I put the wineglass down on a nearby table, which had been carved to resemble a tree stump on a vine base. "I only need one thing from you." With the wineglass out of my hand and distance between us, the fog in my head dissipated. Had there been obfuscation magic in the glass? Clever vamps. I reminded myself to be extra careful and that two—or three—could play this game. I cloaked myself in Fae glamour, putting forth an air of beauty and power...and persuasion.

"No more games," I said. "We both know what we want. I don't want to give you my blood. At the very least I don't want you to bite me—your teeth could scar me."

"I am aware of your concerns, Princess," Ashlee said.

Rae tried to hand me another glass of white wine, and I shook my head. "No, I don't trust you. What wizard do you have working with you to help you with this magic?"

"No tricks, Princess, on my honor," Rae told me. "No magic. No poison. Only wine and glass."

For a vampire to swear by his honor, especially a Japanese vampire, served as an oath, and I couldn't insult him by refusing to accept it. "Thank you." I held the glass for a moment, then took a small, cautious sip. I sensed nothing amiss, not even now that I was alert for the most subtle magic.

"What was that?" I asked Ashlee. "Trying to trick me? To seduce me? I question whether you can even handle the soul-eater."

Her face contorted into a frustrated grimace for a half-second, then smoothed back into her usual cool demeanor. "We can handle him, Princess. Don't worry. The question is, can you handle what you're aiming for once you get it? I've done some digging and have found out about the exiled Fae prince and princess." Then, in a sing-song tone, "I know you're des-per-ate."

Hades, no Fae glamour could remove that knowledge. I allowed the glamour I'd donned to fade slowly so as not to make it too obvious it had been there. "I'm not sure how desperate I am." Oddly, the words rang true, which created the most disturbing moment in the interaction so far. "Or, let me put this a different way, not desperate enough to allow a vampire to drink from me without limits."

Ashlee smiled, and I could tell she'd seen my moment of doubt. Unfortunately, I didn't have time to sort through it all in that moment. Even if—and that was a big, capital IF—I wasn't as eager to return to Faerie as I thought I'd been, we still had to stop the monster and whatever it wanted to do to me because if we didn't, it would hurt more people, including those closest to me.

"What sort of limits?" she asked.

"Ones spelled out in a contract in blood." No supernatural creature could break one of those, although I was sure she'd try.

Her pleasant expression hardened into distaste. "Are you absolutely wedded to that idea?"

"Yes. And I'll write it."

"Very well. I thought you might want something like that, although it's very pedestrian of you, Princess."

Rae brought forth the materials needed—a sheet of vellum, a quill, and a pot of blood. I picked up the quill, dipped it in the pot, and sniffed the end. Yes, human blood. Whatever the level of my desperation, Ashlee wanted to drink from me enough that she wouldn't hold back from my demands.

It had been a while since I'd written my last blood contract, but I remembered the magic. I held the quill over the vellum, and the words streamed forth from it to cover the page. As the words appeared, the level of blood in the pot dropped.

"There," I said and put the quill on the table before stepping back. "You sign first."

She stalked to the table and leaned over the contract, her lips moving as she read. I hid a smile at such a human affectation, but when I glanced at Rae, he held a hand over his mouth, and we shared a small grin. It hit me then—he loved her.

Oooh, that could be a complication because I didn't sense the type of energy between them that would indicate they were lovers.

"You say my part is to capture the soul-eater and one more favor in the future, which you will specify when the time comes, in exchange for one bite not lasting more than two seconds." She frowned at me, and I again had the sense of two predators circling each other.

"That is correct." I shrugged. "You allowed me to write the contract. I can't help but make a Fae bargain." I smiled. "It's in my blood."

She laughed, and the feeling in the room shifted from predatory to gaming. "Very well, Fae. I will accede to your open-ended favor in the future, and I want the bite to last up to ten seconds."

"Four," I countered.

"Six," she retorted, "and that's as low as I'll go."

"All right." I swallowed the upwelling of panic. "Six, and you heal the bite wounds." It had been careless of me to not include that.

"Deal."

I walked back over to the table and held the quill over the contract, then whispered the changes. The letters within the words to be changed untangled themselves, slid around, and re-formed into the terms we had agreed upon. Then I pricked my finger with the quill, allowed a drop of blood to be drawn into the tip, and signed. I stepped away and handed the quill to Ashlee. She pricked her finger and signed as well, and once she lifted her pen, a flash of blue lightning illuminated the terms, and energy snaked between us. Rae rushed forward, and I held up a hand.

When I spoke, the words echoed around the room. "The magic of the contract brooks no interference."

"It's fine, Rae," Ashlee added, and her voice reflected wonderment. "I can see your vessels, Princess. They're calling to me."

I closed my eyes. "Do what we agreed upon."

I thought she would pounce me, but instead, she approached me slowly, licking her lips.

She leaned close to my ear, and the lack of breath on my skin reminded me of her creature type and made me shiver. What had I done?

As if she sensed my regret, she murmured, "I promise you'll enjoy this."

She then led me a few steps to a plush blue fainting couch and guided me to sit supported by the raised side. She put an arm around me and leaned in. Although vampires didn't breathe, she sniffed deeply.

"You smell of wild energy, lighting and thunderous waves," she whispered, and the air she'd inhaled tickled my ear with a cold breeze.

"You don't smell like anything." I'm not sure what I expected —death and decay, maybe? But she was a vampire, not a zombie or other re-animated undead thing. The energy between us allowed me to see her aura, which surprised me with its forest green color.

"We're not all death. Just as you are not all light."

"What...? Never mind, stop talking and just get it over with."

Her teeth pricked the skin over my left carotid artery, the

sharp sting making me gasp. The scientist in me catalogued the sensations—when else would I have this experience? It would allow me to better treat vampire bite victims in the future. She placed her mouth over the holes, and the magic of the contract counted the seconds in my head and the air around us.

One... The natural analgesic property of vampire saliva kicked in, blessedly numbing the puncture wounds. I heard her throat move as she swallowed.

Two... She took a pull, and I held on to the side of the chair as it felt like she took the blood from deep inside my torso rather than my neck.

Three... She snaked her left hand around my waist to hold me steady as my blood flowed into her mouth.

Four... Another pull, and this time I groaned as the pull felt like it came from my groin, filling me with desire.

Five... Almost involuntarily, I clasped her hair, the thick dark strands anchoring me to the present. Pressure, sharp and warm, built between my legs.

Six... The last pull, and I shattered into a trembling orgasm. She swallowed, and she licked the wounds on my neck, which prolonged the sensations, sending another wave crashing through me. Her mouth found mine, and I tasted blood and lust and...something else. Something cold and dark and chaotic. I pulled back.

We sat there and gazed at each other, the haze clearing. I put a hand to my neck and found two slight indentations in the skin.

"A mirror," I gasped and pushed Ashlee off of me. "Someone give me a mirror."

Rae found one in a drawer and handed it to me. I looked at my neck. Two white scars, each the size of the head of a pin, lay where she'd bitten me. Rage burned through the rest of the haze of lust, and I threw the mirror at Ashlee. She caught it deftly and checked her appearance. With a wave of my hand, I made the mirror shatter, and she dropped it.

"That's seven years' bad luck, Princess."

"That's nothing compared to what you just did to me!" I sank to the couch, and wrapped my arms around my stomach, where a pit had opened up. "Don't you know? I can't return to my grandmother's court now. I'm damaged."

"I fulfilled my part. I healed you. The contract said nothing about scarring." Ashlee sashayed over to me and lifted my chin with an index finger. "Don't you know?" she imitated me. "You couldn't have returned anyway. Surely you tasted it in your blood when we kissed—you're not entirely light Fae, like I tried to tell you."

"What do you mean?"

Her lips formed an "o," and then she asked, "Do you know who your father is?"

"No." The words tumbled out of me. "High Fae don't marry like humans do because they don't want attachments and obligations, and when a child is born to royalty, they're considered the child of the court so there are no unnecessary political ties. I'm sure my father is, or was, one of my mother's consorts." I glared up at her, willing her to take her words back. "One of the *light* Fae consorts."

Ashlee put a finger to her lips, and the corners of her mouth curled up into a joker smile. "Keep telling yourself that. I think your mother had a little fun on the side."

I stood and swayed for a second before I found my balance. She'd certainly made the most of her six seconds. She tried to cup my elbow, and I jerked away. "You've done enough."

"Very well." She raised her hands and stepped back. "I believe our business here is done, Princess."

"And what about the soul-eater?"

"I and my team will arrive at the hotel after full dark, when it's safe for us to be out."

The thread of magic from the contract vibrated, and I knew she told the truth. If she'd tried to lie or back out at this moment, the blood contract would take care of her. The question was how she would try to wriggle around within the constraints of the situation. She'd already managed to get away with a technicality on healing versus scarring.

"Very well."

Rae gestured for me to follow him, and he led me down the stairs and back to the door of the club. Although I felt like I'd done the best I could, I still had the sense I'd missed something important. Plus, she must have been mistaken. I was all light Fae. And now I was scarred. Not as badly as Rhys, and I might be able to hide it for a while, but...

First, I'd deal with the soul-eater, and then I'd figure out my next move. Maybe the scars would disappear with time. My self-recrimination never would.

Lawrence waited for me in the convertible, and seeing him made hot tears of shame well up in me. In a weird way, I felt like I'd betrayed him. I should've listened to him, shouldn't have made the bargain with a vampire. How could I have been so stupid? Or—the word came to mind in Ashlee's singsong tone —des-per-ate?

Aria and Kestrel sat in the backseat of his convertible, and none of them appeared happy.

Well, that made four of us.

"And...?" Lawrence asked once I'd gotten in. Sir Raleigh appeared and curled up on my lap. He felt cold again, so I stroked him to warm him. And, truth be told, to calm myself.

I couldn't give him all the details. "She'll meet us with her team at the hotel after full dark. Why are these two here?" I turned to look at the two young women. "I told you I don't want you anywhere near the confrontation with the soul-eater tonight."

"We need to set up our charms around the ballroom and side rooms," Aria replied. "We won't get in the way later, I promise."

Lawrence glowered, and he radiated frustration and general disapproval. No, I wasn't going to tell him what had transpired between me and Ashlee or the scars. I could tell he was in an, *I told you so* mood, and I didn't want to hear it.

"What's our first step when we get to the hotel?" I asked Lawrence.

He answered through a clenched jaw. "We go up to our room and have a chat."

A glance in the rearview mirror at Aria's and Kestrel's guilty expressions made my stomach drop for the second time in an hour. Oh, now I knew what had happened.

"Someone looked back in the scrying bowl, didn't they?" I asked. "Got curious about the visions it had given up today?"

No one would meet my eyes. Lovely.

Finally, Aria said in a small voice, "I had to clear it for one of the charms we were putting together. One of the problems with black quartz is that it's, well, gossipy."

And I could guess exactly what it divulged to the talented witch. Yes, I was in big trouble.

Aria switched to secret conversation, which reminded me of just how powerful she was. *"I didn't tell him anything, just that you two really need to talk. He said he knew. I told him, no, really."*

"Could you at least have waited until after we deal with the soul-eater?"

"If you were in his position, would you want to?"

"No," I had to admit. *"No, I wouldn't."* I texted Rhys to make himself scarce. The last thing I needed was an epic battle between gargoyle and Fae prince, but guess who was waiting for us when we pulled up to the hotel?

21

LAWRENCE

When I'd picked up Kestrel and Aria and helped them put the big cardboard box of stuff in my trunk, I hadn't expected them to have trouble looking at me directly. And I certainly hadn't expected them to be cagey about why, only that I needed to talk to Reine about stuff as soon as possible because she had answers to the questions that had been plaguing me for centuries. I told them I suspected, and we were going to wait until after we'd taken care of the soul-eater, but the thought of them knowing, and Reine knowing, and that little prick Rhys probably knowing... Dammit, if everyone else knew, I deserved to as well.

I'd already been in a pissy mood when we pulled up to the vampire club. Then when Reine came out, her left hand to her neck and her expression despairing, I guessed exactly what had happened. Now she'd be marked, too. Dammit, I'd told her it was a bad idea, that we could figure it out without her having to go to the vamps for help.

The anger that had been simmering and then starting to boil almost reached explosive when Rhys met us at the hotel. His presence wasn't the problem—where else would he be?

No, it was Reine's reaction.

She hopped out of the car almost before it stopped and snapped, "I told you to lie low."

"Why, Reine?" I asked and traded my keys for a valet ticket. "Does he have something to do with what we need to talk about?" I hated being so vague, but no one needed to hear about my drama or witness hers.

I pulled the box from the trunk and handed it to Kestrel, who staggered back from its weight. I took it back. "Let me know where you want this."

"No, Uncle Lawrence, we'll take care of it. We can carry it between the two of us."

Kestrel and Aria did manage to arrange the box so they each held a side. Reine twitched her fingers, and the box shook.

"Thanks," Aria said. "That helps."

"Of course." Reine turned and walked inside, seemingly without care or fear of the soul-eater. That annoyed me even more—was she more eager to face the monster who wanted to kill her than have a conversation with me?

No one said anger was rational. I followed her and Rhys in. Everyone remained silent until we got up to our room.

"Well?" I asked, my arms crossed. "It seems like you two have something to tell me."

Reine sat on the bed and dropped her hand from her neck. I wanted to see the scars, see how bad they were. Irritation at not being able to protect her almost crowded out all the other emotions. Yes, it had been her choice to go to the vampires, but it had also been my failure to keep her safe, no matter what.

Sir Raleigh appeared and slunk under the bed. Smart cat.

Rhys spoke first. "I don't trust you, mate."

Surprise almost made me laugh. "What do you mean, you don't trust me? I've done nothing but take care of your sister. You've only caused trouble."

"Yes, but you're a gargoyle. We all know what your kind does."

"And what is that?"

Rhys pointed to his scar. "This. You make scars. You go back on promises. You fail to do your job, and Fae get hurt!"

"Rhys, enough," Reine said.

"No, when is it going to be enough for you? You don't trust him, either. Otherwise you wouldn't have gone to the vampires and been bitten. I'm not stupid—I know why you're holding your neck. Plus, I feel the contract you signed. How many seconds?"

Reine's shoulders slumped. "Six."

"Six?" Rhys nearly exploded. "You let a vampire suck on you for six seconds?"

A flush crept into her cheeks. "Yes."

Gods, I felt sick to my stomach. Six seconds would mean the loss of a lot of blood. Plus, vampires didn't just drink—they caused their victims' bodies to have a range of reactions. Considering she'd blushed like that for me earlier, I could guess what.

Great, now I could add jealousy to my growing list of uncomfortable feelings.

Rhys apparently had his own set. "And let me guess, you got more than you expected, didn't you? Oh, and by the way, this room smells like sex. Did you let the gargoyle fuck you, sis? Or the vampire? You've had quite the afternoon, haven't you? What would Mum think?"

"Rhys!" She stood and slapped him across his good cheek. "You're out of line."

He put a hand to his face, which must have been stinging. "Don't try to pull that shit on me, Reine. You know you're going to need me, especially once he finds out—"

They both slowly turned toward me as though they'd forgotten I was there. Great, dismissed on top of everything else. I wanted to groan, scream, punch something, perhaps a certain Fae prince who didn't know when to stop talking...

Find out the truth. I wanted to find out the truth, no matter how much it hurt me.

I crossed my arms and summoned my best don't-mess-with-me glower. "Once I find out what?"

They glanced at each other, and seeing them stand there, both facing me, I felt it, two against one. That's what Fae would do, wasn't it? Always stick together. My inner gargoyle stirred, and I had to suppress the urge to shift, to intimidate the answers out of them.

Rhys smiled, but not pleasantly. He pointed to his cheek. "You look a lot like the gargoyle who did this. Your father did, even more so. You gargoyles have strong genetics, you know that?"

"I'm aware." Oh, gods... That last bit of denial, of hope that we could salvage the situation evaporated. Now anxiety joined in the feelings party in my gut.

Rhys continued, "And so when I saw him working on a boat in the river that day, I asked him. He said he didn't remember, but that's what gargoyles do, right? They lie."

"No, not usually," I told him in my most neutral scientist voice. "Not like the Fae."

Rhys shook his head. "Well, whatever. I didn't believe him. So that night, I and a few of my Fae friends went to his house to get the truth from him. Unfortunately, one thing led to another, and..." He shrugged. "Sorry, turns out I was mistaken."

The anger, fear, jealousy, and rage swirled around my torso faster and faster until they contracted in on themselves, a black hole at my solar plexus sucking all possibility of joy or any positive emotion out of my reality. Everything else felt numb like the stone I'd turn into if I failed to resist the urge to stay in my gargoyle form.

"You killed my father." Instead of the satisfaction I thought

I'd have when I found out the truth, I only had more questions. I turned to Reine. "When did you find out?"

She turned her head away. "This morning. I saw the scene in the scrying bowl."

"So, you've known the identity of my father's murderer since this morning. Worse, you knew it was someone here, someone I've been talking to, eating with, almost trusting..." I had to suck in some air to try to lighten the crush of betrayal around my heart and lungs. "I told you last night that this mystery has consumed my entire life, and you didn't tell me right away. And then you didn't tell me this afternoon. You put me off and distracted me by wanting to fool around."

"I wasn't the only one who wanted it!" She blinked, and two tears slid down her face. "And I meant every part of it. Lawrence, I'm falling for you, and I don't know what to do about it."

Why didn't her emotion reach me? Had my heart decided to turn to stone? No, it had only hardened against trusting the person—Fae, not person—who had withheld this information from me. And who would side with her brother against me. That much was obvious.

"I need to go," I said. "I... I need to go."

"Lawrence, wait!" She moved toward me; her arms outstretched. "Please don't. We can figure this out."

"Reine, I need to go."

She stopped and dropped her arms, but for only a second before her left hand found her neck again. She closed her eyes. "Please. I can't lose everything."

"You haven't. You still have your brother. Good luck with that."

And then I left.

~

My footsteps carried me up the stairs. Up and up and up, like I was somehow going to find the Aerie, the place above the world and all the Fae in it, at the top. The sound of ripping clothing barely registered until I reached the door to the roof, which was marked, "Employees Only." I tried the handle, which was locked. Then I tried the key card Jimmy Leak had given me, but it didn't work.

I ripped the handle from the door and kicked it. It flew outward, crashed against the outside stairs, and clattered to a stop halfway up them. After a comically dramatic pause, it slid downward until it lay at my feet.

My gargoyle feet.

I walked up the stairs and stood on the roof, my wings unfurled to test the breeze and the sun beating against my gray skin. I so badly wanted to fly away, but that would be stupid in the daytime. As it was, I shouldn't be up here, shouldn't be showing the world my true form. But I needed it, needed the strength I would get from the sunlight and the open air, the gravel on the surface of the roof...

A cloud covered the sun, and I scowled at the sky. Raindrops pattered around me, and one landed on my face and trailed down my cheek to my mouth. I turned my face upward and opened my mouth to catch the rain. Water spilled over me and into me, and I accepted the cleansing and the benediction.

I knew who had killed my father, the scarred Fae who had appeared on the top of a granite monolith that itself had been scarred with a monument to murder. How had I not made the connection?

Then the woman I thought I was falling in love with had kept the knowledge from me. Not only had she hidden it, she had tried to put off telling me until after we both faced a foe who could potentially prevent me from finding out by killing either or both of us. And then she had almost seduced me.

My gargoyle self laughed, and I had to admit I'd been more

than up for it. In fact, the thought of her supple body against mine and the memory of the sweet taste of her skin made the remnants of my pants tighten.

And then the memory of her betrayal caused me to lose the flash of lust. Why hadn't she told me? To protect her brother. Because if she didn't, she wouldn't be allowed back into Faerie, which was what she truly wanted.

Gargoyles wouldn't be welcome in Faerie, and I didn't want to be with a woman who lied to me even after she'd promised not to, who would sneak out of bed instead of giving me the courtesy of a proper goodbye, who couldn't trust me to figure out how to protect her rather than running to vampires, of all things, who put protecting a little shit of a Fae prince above allowing me the satisfaction of finding out the answer to the question of who killed my father... and who would eventually just disappear into Faerie anyway.

Here I had to admit my own fault. In spite of acting like a scientist who prided himself on observing and accounting for all pertinent variables, I had deliberately ignored the fact that Reine wanted to go back to Faerie above everything else. That she treated the truth according to whether it was convenient for her eventual goal. That while she was attracted to me, I was still a means to an end.

Gods, I'd been so stupid. And I still must be because I wanted to protect her and help her to defeat the soul-eater. Then she could go back to Faerie, vampire bite or no, and I could move on.

If only I could convince myself it would be that easy.

As for Rhys... I would have to figure out how to make sure he faced justice for what he'd done, but that could wait. Revenge would be sweet, and I needed to plan.

22

REINE

"**O**uch!" I pulled my fingers away from the vampire bite scars, which I'd attempted to heal, and which had given me a soul-shock, an electrical shock that zaps one's entire being. I sensed that the blood contract had something to do with it, so perhaps they'd disappear after Ashlee fulfilled her end of the bargain tonight. I hoped so. I thought having the vampire in debt to me and owing me an unspecified favor to be collected later had been clever, but even that had backfired on me.

"You can't really see them," Rhys said and made me jump. I hadn't seen him come into the room. After Lawrence had left, I'd sent Rhys back to his room because I needed to be alone to figure some things out. I'd succeeded in remaining alone, but not in figuring anything out. I conceded Lawrence had every right to be mad at me. I'd been terrible to him, but I'd also been trying to do what I needed to do to get back to Faerie, and I needed his help. Plus, I really did think I could be falling for him. Or had been. It was time to put on my high Fae panties and be grateful I'd managed to drive him away, although I would always regret hurting him.

Right, Fae didn't do regrets, but I certainly had my fair share by now.

"Hey." Rhys gently turned me toward him and examined my neck. "Really, they blend in with your skin."

"But I can feel them. Can't you?"

"No, not really. Something hides your full aura, always has."

"What do you mean?" I walked out of the bathroom. There was no good reason for two people to be in a hotel bathroom at the same time—it was just too small. Well, maybe one reason, but definitely not one I'd want to share with my brother.

"Well, you know how Mum's aura is so bright it's basically like she glows bright blue and Grandmother's is gold? Yours doesn't always come into focus, and when it does, it's not just one color. It's like a soap bubble with lots of stuff swirling around. Whatever the vampire bite has added, it's not obvious."

"How could my aura be more than one color?" I refrained from telling him that his aura was bright-arsed royal purple with a black streak from his injury, which had become a soul-wound.

"I don't know. Has no one ever told you?"

"No, but humans most often can't read us." Or they'd said they couldn't see mine clearly. No one ever told me I had a rainbow.

"Interesting. By the way, are you wearing that?"

"What's wrong with it?" I liked my dress—a low-cut light blue silk gown with a white lace overlay. I'd relented and bought a pair of wings and a flower crown from one of the FaeCon vendors so I could blend in with the fake fairies. The irony wasn't lost on me.

"Aside from the ridiculous wings and fake flowers, you're beautiful. I'll have to beat the men off with a stick." He pantomimed nudging people away, his expression fierce. I laughed, but only for a few seconds. He'd already chased off the one guy I wanted to see me.

"Thanks, I think."

"Hey, cheer up. This time tomorrow you may be home." He sounded wistful.

I gave him a quick hug, then held him at arm's length. His sad expression tugged at my heart. He might be the most annoying being in this realm or any other, but he was still my little brother. "And you may be, too. Grandmother has to let you in since you helped me." Or tried to.

"I guess we'll see."

I touched the scars on my neck again—had they gotten smaller? Rhys moved my hand, lowering it from my neck.

"Stop worrying about them."

I sighed. "I wish I could. But you're right—I have bigger things on my mind. Are you ready?"

He struck a superhero pose, and I giggled. He wore black leather boots, pants, and vest. I'd convinced him to get a pair of bat wings but not anything for his head. I'd be the one chasing off the young women from my dashing brother.

I wished I knew what Lawrence was going to wear. We'd kept the adjoining room door closed after he stalked out so he'd be in control of when we interacted. I'd heard him come in earlier, but I didn't know if he was planning to leave or...or what. Again, my experience with gargoyles was so limited I didn't know what they'd do. But I thought I knew Lawrence the man, and a small part of me hoped he'd still come to the ball and help us capture the soul-eater.

We'd delayed long enough, though. I didn't want the evil creature to think we'd chickened out and start wreaking havoc. Rhys hooked his elbow, and I took his arm. We looked every inch the Fae prince and princess. Well, except for the wings, but what could we do? When in Rome...

I kept glancing behind me at Lawrence's door as we walked to the elevator bay, but he didn't emerge. As we descended and picked up other partygoers, I managed to convince myself that he would be downstairs waiting for us, but again, no such luck.

We followed the crowd to the ballroom, where volunteers checked our badges. Samir came up to us when we walked in. He wore an ornately wrought chain metal vest over a cream-on-cream embroidered shirt and leather trousers. For a second, I thought he was one of my grandmother's guards.

"Looks like Brutus, doesn't he?" I asked Rhys.

"Oddly, yes."

Samir bowed to us, and I curtsied as Rhys made a minimal bend of his waist. "How is security?" I asked. "Has the punch been guarded?"

"It has been taken care of, milady," Samir said with a crooked smile. The role play made me grin back, but then Samir blinked, his face crumpling for a moment into confusion, and Sir Raleigh growled from the reticule hanging at my wrist.

Samir excused himself, murmuring something about having to check on a thing, and every hair on my body stood on end.

So, it was to be like this—stalk and be stalked.

Corvid approached, and Rhys tensed.

"What do you want?" Rhys asked.

Corvid smiled, and this time I recognized the expression as belonging to the soul-eater. I grabbed Corvid's arm and dragged him to the corner of the ballroom.

"I don't know what you want, but you need to leave these people alone."

Corvid laughed, and it wasn't a pleasant sound. It never was when a dark Fae creature spoke through a human.

"Watch and learn, Princess. You can only do so much. By the way, nice vamp bite. I hope she made you scream."

"Thanks. Found some activities to entertain myself with while waiting to take you down." It took strength of will, but I managed not to have our entire plan for defeating the soul-eater come into my head in case he was reading my mind. He had gotten that strong, and when I felt the tendrils of his being trying to creep over from Corvid to me, I let go. He laughed again.

"Whatever your plan is, you're not strong enough to defeat me."

Corvid slumped to the ground as the soul-eater left him, and he collapsed too quickly for me to catch him.

"Some help, please?" I called.

Just my luck, Jimmy Leak ran over from where he'd been talking to the gorgeous woman whom Kestrel had pointed out to me as Samir's wife.

"What did you do to him?"

I straightened. "Nothing! It was that creature I told you about."

"Nice try. Medic!"

Soon we had a group of people gathered around us, and Jimmy had to make them open a path for the EMTs.

Once they'd carted Corvid away, Jimmy wheeled on me. "Look, Doctor River, I agree that there's something strange going on here, and it all seems to start and end with you."

"I had nothing to do with that. Your nephew's less-than-kind spirit made a perfect conduit for the soul-eater."

"You know he's my nephew. That makes your actions personal. Where's the key card I gave you?"

"Right here, why?" I held it up, and he snatched it away. "Hey!"

"I could play along with your game, do what the CPDC wanted me to, but enough is enough."

"Hey, I need that." Otherwise I wouldn't be able to lure the soul-eater into the room where Ashlee and her crew could nab it.

"No, you don't. The last thing I need is for you to be causing more trouble. Now where's your boyfriend? I need to get his key card, too."

A murmuring from the entrance to the ballroom made us both turn.

"He's not my boyfriend, but he is right there."

Indeed, Lawrence strode in. Or, I should say, Lawrence in gargoyle form did, and he headed right toward me. I admired every movement, mostly so I could ignore his scowl.

When he got close enough to speak, the depth of his voice rattled in my chest like loose gravel. "Doctor River, I never told you about the toxicology results."

I looked down at Jimmy Leak, who wouldn't even reach gargoyle Lawrence's chest.

"Are you going to ask for that key card now?" I asked.

"Maybe later," Jimmy squeaked and quickly moved away.

"Was he bothering you?" Lawrence asked.

He was in protective gargoyle mode again. "Not really. What were the results?"

"Aconite alkaloids."

My mind raced with the implications. "So mixed with alcohol, they'd create disinhibition and cracks for the soul-eater to get in. And Samir said the punch had been taken care of, but that was the soul-eater talking. Oh, Hades."

We both ran to the punch table and found the crystal bowl was already more than half-empty. I whispered to the liquid and convinced it to separate so the aconite elements would crystallize and create a residue at the bottom that would be unpleasant to clean, but wouldn't be absorbed into human bodies.

"What did you do?"

"Deactivated the aconite."

"How? Even in solid form, it can be absorbed."

I didn't want to explain to him what I could do, that I had

changed the alkaloids from organic to mineral, so I said, "Pro-prietary Fae information."

"I should've guessed." His growl likely had more to do with his current form than his feelings. At least I chose to think so.

Although I couldn't see it from the ballroom, I sensed the sun dip below the horizon. Sunset. That meant the vampires would be arriving soon, and it was time to lure the soul-eater into the side room for the final battle.

23

REINE

Before I could figure out how to attract the soul-eater and get it to follow me, the deejay allowed the last song to fade into silence and picked up the microphone.

"Good evening, fairy ladies and gentlepersons, welcome to the eighth annual FaeCon ball!"

Everyone cheered and applauded.

"I wanted to let you know we have some special guests this evening, namely a true prince and princess of Faerie. Would Princess Reine and Prince Rhys please come to the stage?"

There was no way he could have known except... when I got close, I saw the red Solo cup on the table beside the turntable, and I had to force myself to keep moving. What in the world was the soul-eater up to?

Rhys and I ascended to the stage from opposite sides, and when I was within reach, I knocked the punch cup off the table. Only a tablespoon or so splashed out. Hades.

"Oh, excuse me, I'm so clumsy," I said.

"Not a problem, Princess." The deejay laughed giddily. "In fact, I invited you up here not so that they could see you, but so you could see what I can do." He held up his arms, and the room went dark. Within a second, a couple hundred cell phone screens illuminated the place.

One girl in the front row held hers under her chin so her face had creepy lighting from below and called in a sing-song voice, "You think you can get away."

"But you can't run forever," a guy behind her, also under-lit, chimed in.

I scooted closer to Rhys. "Oh, Hades, they've all had the punch."

"And you think you can get your allies to help you," a couple in the back crooned.

"But all hope is lost," Samir sang in a baritone I would have enjoyed had the words not been so sinister.

Rhys and I moved toward the edge of the stage as the soul-eater continued its ballad of doom until...

"What's going on?" a panicked voice called from the edge of the room. "No one said anything about a performance!"

"That must be where Kestrel and Aria set up a charm," I told Rhys in the quietest, tightest band of secret communication I could muster.

In fact, they'd set up several. The soul-eater's ballad continued, but it was interspersed with questions and demands for explanations from the edges of the room.

Ah, humans. They did not like surprises. Neither did I.

I reached the side door leading to the room where the punch had been kept, and Lawrence met us there. He and Rhys lifted their chins at each other but thankfully did not exchange words.

The door handle was locked, so Lawrence handed me his card, and I slipped in, followed by the guys.

"Go wait for the vampires at the front and bring them here when they arrive," I told Rhys. He nodded and left through the door to the decorations room.

I trembled at the soul-eater's show of power. I had no doubt he'd fed from each singer, which would make him extremely strong. Strong enough to take over...

I turned to Lawrence, who watched me, his arms crossed and a scowl on his face.

"What?" I asked and edged back toward the decorations room door. "If you're not going to help me, then at least go out there and see if you can assist some very confused 'Con-goers."

"Listen," he said and cupped a massive hand behind one ear.

"What?" I did, but it had gone quiet.

"They're not singing anymore."

Then the *thump-thump-thump* of the regular party music started back up.

"I..."

Lawrence smiled, but it wasn't his smile. I almost didn't recognize it on his gargoyle face. Then his eyes flashed yellow.

No, no, no...

"Let him go! You can't have him!" I launched myself at him, at it, and he batted me away.

I flew several feet and landed against the wall, which thankfully was one of those room divider things, so I ended up doing more of a bounce than a splat. I staggered to my feet beside a fake rock that they'd apparently decided not to use. Too bad it couldn't strengthen me like the real thing.

The soul-eater's laughter sounded even more menacing coming from a gargoyle throat. I gathered all the magic I could and shot a freeze-ball at him, not to hurt him, but to put him into stasis so the soul-eater would be trapped or would let him go. He swatted it back at me, and I ducked and rolled to the side.

Where in Hades were the vampires?

Sir Raleigh emerged from my purse and shifted into his grimalkin form with a low, rumbling growl. He reared back into a pre-pounce shimmy, and I yelled, "No! Don't hurt him, Sir Raleigh."

"No," the soul-eater said in a falsetto, also super creepy coming from a gargoyle, "don't hurt him. Your human side is going to be your undoing, Princess."

I staggered to my feet. "I am a Fae princess."

He laughed again. "That's what you think. If you were a Fae, you wouldn't care what happens to this gargoyle. You're natural enemies, remember?"

"But that wasn't always the case. They used to be our protectors in this realm. *He* used to be my protector." I walked up to him and searched for Lawrence's presence in his eyes. "Lawrence, if you're in there, please help me. You have to fight him. He was able to get in because he possessed you before, but please, please fight him."

He bent his head at an angle, and I stood on tiptoe to press my lips to his.

The words floated into my mind like a thought, *"I'm trying."*

Then the soul-eater's energy slid into my mouth. I drew back and gagged but couldn't get rid of the slimy vine that traveled into my throat and down my esophagus. It sprouted a branch that attempted to pierce my skull, and I screamed around the sensation, but it came out choked, like when I'd been frozen in a nightmare. The vine sent out branches to my organs and my limbs, and I fought it with every ounce of Fae strength I could, but soon it had me on my knees, and my awareness of the room around me flickered.

"You're mine now," it said. *"And soon the throne of Faerie will be mine. Keep feeding me your strength, Princess. That's a good girl. Give it all to me."*

Fighting it made it stronger. But I couldn't give up—so what could I do?

I opened my eyes to see Lawrence kneeling over me, my head cupped in his giant hand.

"Fight it, Reine, don't let it take you."

The sorrow in his voice touched a nerve in my core, and the grasping tendrils of the soul-eater pulled back from it. Interesting...

"I'm sorry," I mouthed, and sorrow flooded through me. "So sorry."

The soul-eater redoubled its efforts, but it felt like it fought the sorrow more than me.

I had been acting the Fae, but what had that gotten me? I'd hurt Lawrence. I'd put myself in a vulnerable position. My actions hadn't gotten me any closer to Faerie.

So how much of a human side did I have? I searched my heart for the things that made humans what they were—vulnerability, true cooperation, love, grief... I thought about how Lawrence and I had shared our stories and our pain, how Kestrel and Aria had worked together and how I wanted to help Kestrel figure out her magic, how I truly did love Sir Raleigh even if I couldn't quite figure out who he worked for. How I grieved over the chance with Lawrence I'd thrown away because I'd been too cowardly. It hadn't been fear that he'd make me choose between him and Rhys—he valued family too much for that—but that I wouldn't be up to supporting him like he'd need amid my conflicting feelings. For a Fae, I hated drama.

My embracing of my human weakness had also weakened the soul-eater, but I couldn't expel it. I needed one more push, one more major emotional, vulnerable moment.

It had one more attack, though. The image of my mother came to mind, and she said to someone I couldn't see, *"I am so disappointed in Reine. She's become one of them. You don't deserve to return to Faerie."*

That activated my old defenses—I did, too, deserve to return to Faerie. I was a freaking Fae princess!

The soul-eater started growing inside me again, and I had

to do something quickly. I opened my eyes again and looked straight at Lawrence. "I can't believe I'm saying this, but I think I may be falling in love with you."

Lawrence shook his head and turned his head away. "I... I don't know what to feel or think, Reine."

His rejection and the regret for my part in it hit me right in the gut, and the emotional agony spread through my entire body. The soul-eater drew in on itself. White-hot pain sparked in every cell as it released them. I rolled away from Lawrence to my side and retched. With a full-body heave, I expelled the soul-eater, which I'd withered with my vulnerability to a black worm, like an evil vanilla bean.

The door burst open, and Ashlee, Rae, and two more vampires came in, followed by Rhys. They surrounded the soul-eater on the floor, and Ashlee laid a handkerchief spun of lace so fine it resembled spider silk over it. The edges moved in as the center ballooned up until it completely encased the soul-eater. Ashlee picked it up.

"Good grief, Princess, what did you do to it?"

"I fed it with my humanity. That weakened it."

She raised her perfect eyebrows. "I didn't think you had it in you."

"Yes, I do. Even if it disappoints everyone around me." I knelt and then allowed Lawrence to help me to my feet. "Thank you for taking that thing. Please be sure to keep it contained."

Ashlee smiled—thankfully her own. "Oh, believe me, I will. And you're welcome. I'll wait for your call for the favor that will satisfy our contract."

"Perfect." She and I shook hands, and the vampires left, leaving me with Lawrence and Rhys.

"Rhys, could you excuse us?" I asked.

Rhys, contrary to his usual MO, did not argue. "Sure, I'll go see what damage control needs to be done." Then he walked back into the ballroom.

Ashlee poked her head back around the door and gestured for me to join her in the next room.

"By the way, thought you might like to know that your brother delayed us coming to help you. Otherwise, I would've been there to help you get rid of the thing. You still have some of its residual energy around you." She cocked her head. "Or maybe that's some of your own dark Fae energy."

I didn't want to get into that discussion right now. "He delayed you? How?"

"He sent us to the wrong part of the hotel first, then pretended to have gotten lost." She inclined her head toward the punch room. "Stick with the gargoyle. He's a good one. Your brother..."

"...is a Fae, and Fae always have complications within subplots within games." I sighed. "Thank you for letting me know."

"You're welcome." Her smile told me she enjoyed this way too much. Who had Ashlee Wyatt been before she'd become a vampire? I guessed she'd been a noble in some royal court known for deep intrigue.

I returned to find Lawrence still in gargoyle form.

"I guess this is it," Lawrence said. "You're going to return to Faerie, aren't you?"

I placed my hands on his smooth pecs and gave him my most genuine pleading expression. "Not unless I have something to stay for here."

He gently removed my hands from his body and held them palm-to-palm in his own. "Go, Reine. You've wanted this too badly to give it up." Then he stepped back and out of the room, leaving me with a lump in my throat and a closed door between us.

24

REINE

I didn't return to the ball. Nor did I go up to the hotel room. I knew what I'd find up there—Lawrence either packing or already gone, and I couldn't take more rejection. I'd already told him how I felt. Twice, actually, and he obviously didn't return the feelings. Whatever he'd felt for me before, I'd hurt him too deeply and killed it.

With the soul-eater contained, I figured it would be safe to take a walk into the wooded area by the hotel, where the soul-eater had attacked me on my first day in Atlanta. I allowed my footsteps to meander on the path and drew strength from the trees and then the stream. Nothing lightened the sorrow in my heart, either over Lawrence or Rhys having betrayed me. Why had I expected anything different? I'd have to talk to Rhys eventually, but I had reached the end of my emotional strength. At least the cat still liked me. Sir Raleigh, back in cat form, padded along beside me, although occasionally he stopped and sniffed the air.

"Are you expecting someone?" I asked.

He never answered.

Once I reached the bottom of the hill, I sat on a wrought-iron bench by the stream and closed my eyes so as to better experience the breeze and the night sounds. Homesickness flooded through me, and again, it felt more like longing for my little cottage in the Scottish Highlands. But then when I probed the emotions, I found them to be grief for the life I thought I'd had, my somewhat predictable solo Fae existence where I knew I'd get back to Faerie eventually, and in the meantime, I knew what to expect. In spite of my exile, my place in the world had seemed secure, and I'd felt far away from the political machinations of Faerie. Plus, I hadn't started to fall for a handsome gargoyle who had a tragic connection to my family.

But I hadn't had a cat or a grimalkin, and Sir Raleigh curled up on my lap and purred. I opened my eyes when he chirped and stroked his soft fur. He rolled over to show me his belly.

"Farthing for your thoughts?" a male voice asked.

Ellerin appeared, already sitting, on the bench beside me. Sir Raleigh let out an excited squeak and stretched, and then the little traitor pushed his head under Ellerin's hand. With a grin, Ellerin scratched Sir Raleigh's head, and the cat purred and walked back and forth across Ellerin's lap.

"That although I've managed to end up with a broken heart and am not sure what I want anymore, I at least have a grimalkin who likes me."

Ellerin chuckled. "Yes, these wee creatures bring a lot of comfort, don't they?"

"That they do. Thank you for sending him to me."

Ellerin turned to me and raised his eyebrows. "And what else have you figured out, lass?" His eyes crinkled at the corners when he smiled, but that didn't stop the shock of familiarity or the realization that came with it.

"Not much. You and I are related somehow—we have the exact same color and shape eyes—and you and my grandmother are up to something."

He looked down at Sir Raleigh, who blinked innocently.

"I told you not to bring her into the Gray Zone," Ellerin said. Sir Raleigh yawned, and Ellerin sighed. "That's the problem with choosing a cat form for your grimalkin—they do have their own minds."

"Who are you?" I asked.

"Someone who wants to help." He stood and held out a business card. "I know you're hoping your mother will let you back into Faerie. I can assure you that's highly unlikely. It's time to stage your return on your own terms, Princess. Call me when you're ready."

I took the card. The words in elegant scripted font read: Ellerin Fae, LLC, Guide to the Shadowed Path.

The Shadowed Path, the legendary secret way into Faerie that went through the Dark Forest and the Gray Zone, existed? I should've guessed. With a shiver, I said, "There's no phone number."

"You don't need one to reach me. You can ask him." He nodded to the cat and disappeared.

"Well, at least I know who you've been working for," I said to Sir Raleigh. He jumped down from my lap and started up the path. "Right. I guess it is time to go."

THE NEXT MORNING at five minutes before sunrise, I stood with my suitcase and Sir Raleigh at the top of Stone Mountain in the clearing where the veil between this realm and others had thinned. Kestrel had given me a ride, and we'd said goodbye at the bottom of the mountain.

"Will I see you again?" she asked through tears. "I thought we were going to keep training."

"Maybe," was all I could say. "I'm sure that even if I can't, you'll find someone who can." In truth, I still didn't know why she couldn't settle into any one set of powers.

She hugged me, which surprised me, and I hugged her back.

"And don't worry about Uncle Lawrence," she said. "He'll come around."

"I don't think so, but thanks."

So now I stood, waiting for my mother to appear. At one minute before sunrise, Rhys walked over the hill.

"'Ello, Sis," he said. "Tried to text you, but you didn't answer."

I turned away from his attempt at a hug. "I know what you tried to do."

He didn't deny anything. I didn't expect him to. That was the story of my life—when you counted on someone, they'd just turn against you eventually. And I'd screwed things up with the one person—gargoyle—who never would have.

The air in front of us shimmered, and the temperature rose by a few degrees. Whereas before, the morning had been redolent with the scents of damp rock and earth as well as green growing things, now the sweet aromas of flowers that had never grown on earth teased my nose with promises of home. My mother appeared in her favorite dress of light blue, and she wore a crown of real flowers on her head. A small part of me, the little girl who had always wanted her approval, searched her face for some sign of happiness and pride. The rest of me was unsurprised to find only coldness and...anger? What could she be angry about?

"Mother," Rhys said, and he smiled at her. "You look lovely today."

"You failed," she said.

"We didn't fail," I argued. "We stopped the soul-eater and made sure it will be contained. That was the last loose end."

"And did you find out where it came from?"

"No, other than a collaboration of a light and a dark Fae in Faerie." Some instinct stopped me from saying more.

"Then you haven't tied things up, have you, Daughter?"

I sighed. "It would be easier for me to investigate if I could actually, you know, get into Faerie."

"I'm sorry, but no."

"You're not sorry," I said. "And even if I do find this out, you're not going to let me return. Why don't you tell me what this is really about?"

"Fine, if you don't want to come home, you don't have to, you ungrateful child. Your opportunity is rescinded."

I almost argued, almost pleaded. Almost cried. But instead, I straightened my spine and lifted my chin. "I am a princess of Faerie. You cannot keep me from my home forever."

If I didn't know her so well, I would've missed the fear that flashed across her face. I'd seen it before. She wasn't afraid of the soul-eater, but something else.

"What about me?" Rhys asked. "You said if I helped, I could return, too."

"You failed as well, Son."

Then she disappeared.

I turned to Rhys. "And what exactly did you fail at, Rhys? Sabotaging me? Keeping me from defeating the soul-eater?"

He shook his head. "I'm not going to say. It sounds like we need to make some plans."

"Not we, *me*. *I'm* going to plan. You're going to go crawl back under whatever rock you came from and get the hell out of my life."

He didn't try to stop me as I walked back to the gondola station.

"What are you going to do?" Kestrel asked as she pulled out of the park and headed toward Highway 78.

I pulled out Ellerin's card. "I'm going to sneak into Faerie."

She shot me a skeptical glance. "Isn't that impossible?"

"No, but it's very dangerous. There's a way called the Shadowed Path, which is basically a back door in through the lands of the dark and gray Fae." I knew Ellerin could find his way around, and I suspected Sir Raleigh could, too.

"I'm coming with you. It will be an adventure."

"Um, no, young lady. I think not. It's too risky."

"But wouldn't Faerie be one place where I could possibly figure out my powers? Nothing here is going to work. Trust me, my mom tried. She died trying. I owe it to myself to do whatever it takes."

I started to argue, but she had a point. If I could make it back to my grandmother's court and—even better—into my grandmother's good graces, we could have our Fae physician examine her. And he would be much more likely to cooperate if she had assisted me in my return.

No, it was too dangerous, but I couldn't take any more arguing. At least I knew there was no way her father would agree, and he might be the last one I had access to who could influence her. "Let me talk to your dad about it."

She snorted. "He won't let me. Please, Reine."

"First we talk to him."

"Fine, we'll go there now."

She drove to her father's house, and we found him at the kitchen table drinking coffee. The weight of grief shrouded his energy, but he smiled when he saw us.

"Good morning, Doctor River," he said.

"Good morning, Doctor Graves."

Kestrel practically bounced on her toes. "Dad, we have a proposition for you. Something that could help me with my magic."

"Oh?"

We laid out the plan, and then I paused, waiting for his refusal. Hoping for his refusal, if I was going to be honest. I didn't know what Ellerin would charge me to sneak into Faerie. I didn't know if I could afford passage for two.

"Yes, on one condition," he said.

"What?" I asked as Kestrel shouted, "Yay!"

"That I come with you."

25

LAWRENCE

After rejecting Reine, I'd gone back to the room, changed back to human, and left the hotel before I could find Rhys and...what? As much as I wanted to take my revenge on him, once I regained control of my logical faculties and thought through the potential repercussions, I knew going after Rhys wouldn't help. It wouldn't bring my father back, and I might start something worse between the Fae and my people. So, I dropped those plans, as I had other dreams, desires, and hopes.

On Sunday, I went through the motions of getting ready for the week, but my brain remained in a fog, and the grief over the losses of the past week weighed me down. I thought that once I knew the truth about my father's death, I would be happy. I could move on and devote the entirety of my mental resources to my research. Or maybe I could date, find a companion to spend part of my long life with. The latter no longer sounded as exciting as it had when I'd thought about it before. Not now that I'd tasted the kisses of a certain green-eyed Fae. I hoped she had gotten what she wanted.

Would I feel it when she left this realm for Faerie? Did I want to?

When I walked out to my driveway to get into my sensible sedan to go to my sensible job on Monday morning, I found a surprise waiting for me. Rhys pushed himself off from where he'd been leaning against a tree and approached. I waited until he got within arm's length, and then I punched him. He staggered back, clutching his face.

He moved his jaw, then said, "I suppose I deserved that. What are you, made of rock?"

I flexed my fingers. All right, that had been satisfying. "What do you want?"

He pointed to my phone, which stuck out from my right hip pocket and buzzed with a text. He asked, "Heard the news from work yet?"

"What do you mean?"

Then I saw the text from Linda, one of the lab assistants: *Doctor John Graves is going on an unspecified leave of absence. Wanted to give you a heads-up before you get here.*

"How did you know? And, more importantly, why do you care? Believe me when I say you are literally the last person on earth I want to see."

"Even more than my sister?"

I sighed. "My feelings for her are none of your business."

"But you do have feelings for her."

"Again, why do you care? You said you didn't trust me." I moved to walk around him, but he blocked me. "Don't make me hit you again."

"Look, mate, I don't like you, but I saw how you took care of her when she was attacked. The whole time, really, and I know I can trust you...*with her*. That's why I'm here."

Anxiety hollowed out a place in my stomach. "What's happened?"

Rhys glanced over his shoulder, then back at me. "I've screwed up royally. More than before."

"What did you do now?"

"She's about to walk into a trap. She and a Fae named Ellerin are going to sneak into Faerie on the Shadowed Path, but her enemies will be waiting."

"How do you know this, and what do you expect me to do about it? I can't go into Faerie."

"She's brought two humans with her. There will be a brief window where other creatures can get in, too."

The text took on a more sinister context. "Which two humans?"

"That cute little redhead Kestrel and her father."

The thud of my briefcase as it hit the ground alerted me that I'd dropped it. "Stones. How much of a head start do they have?"

"So, you'll go after them with me?"

It occurred to me that this could be a trap for me—or us—as well, but... "Yes. I can't let anything happen to John and Kestrel."

"And Reine."

"Right, and Reine."

"Good. Here's what you'll need..."

DID YOU LOVE SHADOWS OF THE HEART?

Thank you for reading Shadows of the Heart! If you'd like to be alerted as to when it's available, please join my Fae Files VIP newsletter list at https://www.subscribepage.com/faefilesnews

Here's something you're probably seeing at the end of a lot of books: a plea for reviews. That's because they help our books to be found and helps other readers know they're good. Also, some major vendors only start showing books to potential readers when they have a certain number of reviews.

I would be so grateful if you'd leave a review at the site where you bought the book or on Bookbub or Goodreads, and, if you're feeling frisky like Sir Raleigh on catnip, other places, too. Thanks so much!

Be careful what you wish for...

The end of my exile and my return to Faerie aren't going as I imagined. First, I have to sneak in rather than enter in triumph.

This means traveling the shadowed paths typically forbidden to those of the Light Court.

Second, I need to figure out what to do with a certain handsome gargoyle, who still hasn't forgiven me or my brother for a major betrayal.

Third, someone in my grandmother's court is trying to kill me.

If I don't outwit my hidden but clever pursuer, I'm guaranteed to lose everything in the final battle against the powerful enemy who's been pulling the strings all along.

The Shadowed Path *is the third installment of The Fae Files, a series with magic, wit, and a little bit of bite. If you like snarky hero-ines, memorable creatures, and unique magical worlds, then you'll love Cecilia Dominic's spellbinding series.*

The Shadowed Path can be ordered from your favorite online retailer or from your local bookstore via Ingram. You can ask them to look it up with the ISBN 978-1-945074-66-0

ABOUT THE AUTHOR

By day, clinical psychologist Cecilia Dominic helps people cure their insomnia. By night, this USA Today bestselling urban fantasy and steampunk author writes fiction that keeps her readers turning pages past bedtime. She prefers the term "versatile" to "conflicted" and has published both short story and novel-length fiction. She lives in Atlanta, Georgia, with her husband and the world's cutest cat.

Read more from author Cecilia Dominic at:

ceciliadominic.com

~

Sign up for Cecilia's newsletter and get a novella at the following link:

https://www.subscribepage.com/CeciliaDominicbackofbook

If you'd like to be added to a special list just for Fae Files updates, please go to https://www.subscribepage.com/faefilesnews

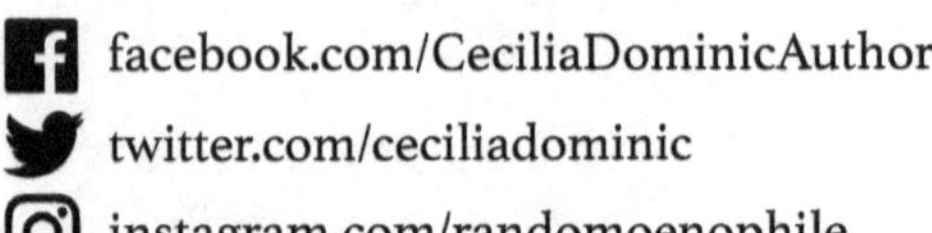

facebook.com/CeciliaDominicAuthor

twitter.com/ceciliadominic

instagram.com/randomoenophile